# And They Lived....
# Ever After

CW01455881

# And They Lived... Ever After

## Disabled Women Retell Fairy Tales

HarperCollins *Publishers* India

First published in India by HarperCollins *Publishers* 2024
4th Floor, Tower A, Building No. 10, DLF Cyber City,
DLF Phase II, Gurugram, Haryana – 122002
www.harpercollins.co.in

2 4 6 8 10 9 7 5 3 1

This anthology copyright © Rising Flame 2024
Preface copyright © Rising Flame
Individual stories copyright © respective authors

P-ISBN: 978-93-5699-640-3
E-ISBN: 978-93-5699-674-8

This is a work of fiction and all characters and incidents described in this book are the product of the author's imagination. Any resemblance to actual persons, living or dead, is entirely coincidental.

Each individual writer asserts the moral right to be identified as the author of their work.

All rights reserved. No part of this publication may be reproduced, stored in a retrieval system, or transmitted, in any form or by any means, electronic, mechanical, photocopying, recording or otherwise, without the prior permission of the publishers.

Typeset in 11.5/15 Adobe Garamond at
Manipal Technologies Limited, Manipal

Printed and bound at
Replika Press Pvt. Ltd.

FSC
MIX
Paper from
responsible sources
FSC® C016779
www.fsc.org

This book is produced from independently certified FSC® paper to ensure responsible forest management.

*This book is dedicated to women with disabilities,*
*chronic illnesses and mental health conditions living across the world*

# Contents

*Preface*                                                          ix

The Ugly Duckling                                                   1

Rapunzel and the People of Companara                               20

It's Still Your Choice                                             34

Cinderella's Sister                                                55

Beat-Matching Beethoven                                            69

The Ugly Duckling                                                  86

The Deaf Snow White                                                97

Agal                                                              109

Quack                                                             124

Maryam and the Moon Angel                                         145

The Swan in Disguise                                              157

Red                                                               175

The Witch                                                         185

*About the Anthology Process*                                     199
*About the Organization*                                          201
*Acknowledgements*                                                203

# Preface

WE HAVE GROWN UP WITH FAIRY TALES ALL AROUND us. From the movies we watch to the books we read to everyday metaphors, these stories shape our ideas, and show us who we want to be, who exists in the world, what kind of love we imagine and how we want the stories of our lives to go. But not all of us get to see ourselves in these stories. Children and adults who live with disabilities usually find that characters like them are absent in fairy tales and when present they are often depicted as scary, evil characters out to harm others. Through this they (and all of us) learn that facial scars, deformities and limb differences are all things to fear—be it the Hunchback of Notre Dame or Scar in *The Lion King*, or the Beast in *Beauty and the Beast*. In many ways, these stories we've heard from time immemorial tell us about how we, as a society, perceive worth and value, who we wish happy endings for and who are kept away from these emotions.

This collection aims to change that. We recognize the potential of fairy tales and their ability to build our worldview, to shape how we perceive love, life, community and belonging. Through these powerful retellings we find community in the Ugly Duckling story, have 'Rapunzel' demand a better world for herself, have 'Cinderella' find self-love, and 'Snow White' find those she can be herself with. These stories, rewritten by thirteen disabled women, infuse our age-old fairy tales with agency, joy, love and compassion. Through each retelling, we find our way to new possibilities of belonging in this world; we visualize and see the colours and experiences and lives of people who are not often thought of. All the while providing new representation and hope for a new generation of disabled people.

Though this book was put together keeping in mind the wide gulf of missing stories of women with disabilities, what we found while working on them is that they provide us, as a society, with new and fresh ways of seeing the world. They bring each of us—disabled and non-disabled—closer to the reality that the world is diverse and that we can all bloom when differences are supported and not stigmatized. They hold close our experiences of being misfits, of self-doubt, isolation, bullying and discrimination. These stories teach us of more than one way of living life and how love, empathy, acceptance and friendship can bring us closer.

As women with disabilities reauthoring these stories, we see the everyday reality of persons across disabilities reflected in these fairy-tale worlds; all while we see disabled women dreaming and living their lives, their experiences of rejection and resilience, their wisdom of innovating and courage of altering lives around them, and finding ways of healing and thriving.

We invite you to read these stories and share them with others who might find solace and connection between these pages and walk together into the worlds imagined.

# The Ugly Duckling

## *by Priyangee Guha*

ONCE UPON A TIME, IN A LAND FAR, FAR AWAY, TWO young ducks—Suri and Geet—were looking for a place to build a nest and start a family together. As they wandered around, they found a quaint corner covered with huge leaves beside a lake. This lake was surrounded by large trees. There was a flowerbed near it where daffodils of all shapes, sizes and colours were blooming.

This lake was very popular among the ducks. They all came here for a swim every day. The water in the lake was known for its natural sweetness and healing power.

'It is a miracle that this space is empty,' Suri observed. 'This is perfect. The huge leaves will keep our nest dry, and the tree branch will give us privacy and protection.'

'We can teach our children how to swim in this lake, and watch the sun rise and set every day. Oh! I can totally imagine what a lovely family home this will be,' Geet said excitedly.

The nest was ready just in time for Geet to lay her eggs. The couple were very happy.

'It is the most beautiful set of eggs!' Suri exclaimed.

Geet gently sat on the eggs to keep them warm. They were looking forward to welcoming their little ducklings.

'Remind me, honey,' she asked after a week, 'how many days did Old Lady Duck say I should warm the eggs before they hatch?'

'Twenty-eight days, plus-minus a week. It apparently varies from egg to egg.'

'I wonder how long you will take?' she absent-mindedly asked the eggs.

Then Geet noticed something she had not noticed earlier.

'Honey, do you think this one egg is larger than the others?'

'Don't worry! You are tired. Just try to nap while you warm. You will need all the energy when they are born.'

'You are right.'

She went back to warming the eggs, and tried to keep her anxious thoughts at bay.

'Twenty-eight days?' she muttered. 'I wonder how long that is.'

～

Thirty days later.

'I am so tired, I cannot sit on these eggs anymore! Why are they not hatching?' Geet said all flustered.

'Maybe I should go talk to Old Lady Duck and see if she can give us give some tips.'

'Let's wait for another day or two. She is a little judgmental. She will blame me for having children this late in life. If they don't hatch by then, we will call on her.'

Saying that, she closed her eyes. Suri understood what it meant. He went away to the pond for a swim while keeping a close watch on her in case she needed help. After about an hour, he heard a loud squeal from the nest. He quickly walked up to see an egg beginning to crack a little, and a tiny fluffy yellow head pop up.

'She is beautiful,' he said, tearing up.

As soon as he finished that sentence, he noticed another egg crack, and a little duckling popped up again. This time it was a boy. One by one all the eggs except one hatched.

'Oh, how lovely they look. These two have your eyes,' he said lovingly.

'And these two have yours.'

'What should we name them?' he asked.

'What about Meher and Rusha for the girls?'

'Oh I love them. What about Sahir and Riaan for the boys?'

'Perfect.'

Right then, they realized that the fifth egg—the large one—had not hatched. They stood there in silence. Suri knew that Geet was tired, so he wanted to tread lightly.

After a while, she said, 'Why is this one not hatching?'

'Maybe it needs more heat because it is slightly bigger?'

'Maybe. I did say I will try for another day or two. Let's wait and see what happens.' She closed her eyes again.

'As you wish, my love. Meanwhile, I will take care of the four of them. You focus on this egg for now.' Saying this, he left to take care of the newborn ducklings.

They were yellow as fresh sunshine, with a soft covering of down. They were huddled together with their eyes closed. Suri sat there admiring their beauty. It started to rain, so he pulled the branch with large leaves and covered them properly.

The following morning, they woke up to the lovely smell of petrichor. It had rained all night. The flowers seemed bigger and brighter. Birds were chirping, squirrels were running up and down the tree branches, and the ducks had come back to the lake for a swim. They loved the lake after a fresh rain. The sky was clearer, and there was a lovely rainbow.

'I wish I could swim too,' Geet sighed while contemplating calling for Old Lady Duck.

As evening rolled in, she was about to give up, when she felt something. She looked at the egg, and sure enough the egg started to hatch. She excitedly called her husband.

'It is happening! Oh, how beautiful this is!' he exclaimed.

After what seemed like hours, a head emerged, followed by the rest of the body. They were shocked. She looked nothing like her other siblings. She was not yellow, but the colour of dust. She did not have a soft down like her siblings. She did not quack like them either.

'What is that?'

'I don't know.' Suri tried to say something more articulate but could not.

'I have never seen anything like this. It is so ugly!'

While Geet and Suri were arguing, they did not notice that the little one was shivering with fright. She was just born, and instead of being celebrated, all she witnessed was anger and hate. She could not understand what was happening. But at that very moment, she knew she was not wanted. She was an outcast. She was an imposter.

∼

For two whole weeks, Geet and Suri refused to acknowledge the presence of their fifth duckling. They 'forgot' to take her for swims. They 'forgot' to feed her on time. They did not even name her.

She spent most of her time alone. Her favourite place was a tree in the farthest corner of the lake with big, heavy leaves. No one went there and she enjoyed the silence. It was away from the nests so she could not hear anyone, or smell any food, or get prodded and poked. One day, she was quietly sitting there and playing with an abandoned soft toy that she had found nearby. She was singing her favourite nursery rhyme on loop.

*'Yankee Doodle went to town*
*riding on a pony.*
*He stuck a feather in his hat*
*And called it macaroni.'*

She loved repeating songs, words, phrases—anything. Repeating the same thing made her feel relaxed and calm.

'Oye! What are you doing here alone?'

She nearly jumped out of her skin. She was not expecting company, and certainly not Old Lady Duck, who made fun of everything about her—how she looked, how she talked, how she walked.

'How many times will you sing the same song? Go learn something new, will you?'

'But I love this song. I don't want to learn a new one.'

'And what are you so startled about? You look like you just saw a ghost!'

'No, I just did not expect someone here. So when you suddenly spoke, I got a little frightened.'

'Frightened?' Old Lady Duck laughed out loud. 'Hey listen, everyone,' she called to the other ducks. 'This little Kaali was frightened because I said Hi to her. Can you believe this? You are getting quirkier every day. How will you survive real scary things in life if a simple Hi scares you this much?'

Everyone started to laugh.

As if on instinct, she clutched the toy closer to her and started stepping backwards slowly. She wanted to get smaller and smaller and disappear.

'Oh, this one time she got startled when I jumped into the lake,' Old Lady Duck added. This led to more laughter.

'And the other day, she was rocking back and forth with her ears closed because we were singing at a wedding,' another added.

'Hey, Geet, how did you manage to give birth to such a weird child? She is nothing like you or Suri,' Old Lady Duck sneered.

'Well, I am not even sure she is ours.'

'What have you named her, by the way?'

'Do I look like I care? Let's just forget about her and enjoy our swim, shall we?'

'You have to give her a name. She will need that in school. Unlike the old days, you cannot leave her out of school. Apparently, it is compulsory.'

～

After two weeks of denial, Geet and Suri begrudgingly came to terms with the fact that they had to raise their fifth duckling or get arrested for child abuse.

'What do you want to call that thing?' Suri asked.

'I don't know. Just decide something. I don't care', Geet replied.

Sahir, overhearing the conversation, blurted out, 'Old Lady Duck calls her Kaali, you know.'

'Everyone should call her Kaali then,' Geet said.

'Kaali, Kaali, Kaali, Kaali ...' the other children started singing in chorus and poked their sister with a small branch.

'Stop, please stop,' she pleaded, 'Mom, Dad, please make them stop.'

She covered her ears and curled up, making herself smaller and smaller. 'Dear God, make it go away. Make the noise go away. Make me go away,' she repeatedly muttered under her breath. The smell of food and loud conversation at the same time was a lot to process. The constant poking by her four siblings made her shrivel up in fear. She was nauseous. She felt like the world around her was spinning really fast. When she couldn't take it anymore, she ran out of the nest and hid under the largest and the heaviest leaf of her favourite tree. The weight of the leaf gave her comfort, like a warm hug. 'ten-nine-eight-seven-six-five-four-three-two-one, ten-nine-eight-seven-six-five-four-three-two-one...' she chanted on loop to calm herself down. She did not emerge until she was sure all four of her siblings had gone to bed. And then, she tiptoed to the nest. Everyone was asleep. She could hear her parents snoring. She looked around for food, but everything was over. She saw a small worm wiggle around and ate it up quickly. But she was still hungry, and also tired. She gradually fell asleep while her stomach grumbled loudly.

The next day, she woke up before all her siblings. Her parents were awake, and were sitting by the lake. They seemed to be in the middle of a conversation.

'Everyone got the letter. This lake is of historical importance. No one is allowed to live on its bank anymore. Don't worry, I already found a larger nest near your parents' nest,' she heard her father say.

*Oh no! I hate new places. They make me nervous. I was just getting used to this place. I have my favourite corners, trees, leaves. How will I learn to adjust in a new place? Why do we have to move?* Kaali's thoughts were spiralling when she heard her mother say, 'Wonderful. It is in a nice school district.'

'Are you sure they are ready? Don't you think it is too early?'

'No, these days ducklings go to school earlier. It is more competitive later. I will arrange a meeting with the principal today. The new academic session starts next week.'

'Kaali?'

'What about her?'

'Will she go too?'

'She will have to. It is compulsory. Besides, with the way she looks, education is the only way she can get ahead in life. We have no choice but to take her too.'

While the conversation made her sad, she was also excited about going to school. It meant she would have a routine to follow instead of loitering around alone. She was excited to learn how to swim, fish and quack-sing.

~

It was the ducklings' first day at school. They all woke up early, giddy with excitement. Unlike other mornings, everyone showered without much protest and sat down to eat breakfast.

'Now remember, school is very important. I want you to listen to your teachers. I do not want to hear any complaints about any one of you. Do you understand?'

'Mother?' Meher asked.

'Yes?'

'Do we have to go with Kaali? Can she not go to the other school?'

'No, she cannot. I do not have time to do multiple school trips.'

'But...'

'No more questions. Now go get your bags.'

They often talked about her like she was not in the room. She was used to it. Today, nothing could bother her. She was going to school—away from home. She was tired of being poked and prodded. She was tired of always hiding from her family. Today she was determined to make friends. Even though she was clueless about how to 'make friends' or what friendship felt like. She neatly packed her pencil box—five pencils sharpened and arranged by size, two erasers, one sharpener and two notebooks. She made an older duck tell her all about schools and teachers and made meticulous mental notes. Nothing would go wrong today. Nothing *should* go wrong today. She was nervous about going to a new place, but excited too.

They left for school after breakfast. Her siblings maintained a safe distance from her. She was used to that too. They did not want anyone to associate them with her. When she reached the school, a tall and slim white duck with large rimmed glasses greeted them.

'Welcome to Daisy Duck International School. We are very happy to have you here. Thank you, parents. We will take your children from here. Please come back on time to pick them up.'

She escorted a group of students to the school. As they started walking, Kaali was too distracted to realize that everyone was avoiding her. Her school had an overbearing smell of disinfectant. Ever since the pandemic, all public places smelled like that. She hated that smell. It made her head hurt. The fact that this was an unknown place made it much worse. She clutched her bag closer to her body and hugged it like a pillow.

'Daisy Duck International School. Daisy Duck International School. Daisy Duck International School,' she chanted on loop. Repeating the same phrase always calmed her down and helped her from spiralling into anxious thoughts.

As she calmed down a little, she noticed that all her classmates were looking at her and muttering among themselves.

'Look at how she is walking...'

'Look at how she looks!'

'Why is she flapping like that?'

'Why is she holding her bag like that?'

Everyone was looking in her direction. Her siblings looked positively aghast and were trying to avoid eye contact with her.

*I don't even know why I expected them to protect me*, Kaali thought.

Meanwhile, the teacher who was escorting them stopped abruptly. Some of the ducks stumbled.

'Now, let me show you around the school. That large field with trimmed grass is where you will learn how to walk. No one likes a duck without grace. When you go to middle school, the grass will not be trimmed and you will have to walk amidst different hurdles.

That clear lake over there is where you will learn how to swim. That open arena over there—you will learn how to fly there,' she said.

'For those of you who have an interest in music, your music lessons will be conducted there.' She pointed in the direction of an area filled with musical instruments, marked by a signpost that said 'Quack-sical Corner'.

'Your first lesson is: How to quack like a duck, and your teacher is waiting over there. Go on, don't waste time!'

They walked up to the classroom and everyone hurried to get good spots. The hustle and bustle made Kaali nervous. She stood in one corner covering her ears, with her eyes shut tight. When she opened her eyes, she saw that everyone had settled down in their place of choice and realized no one wanted to be near her.

'Settle down please,' the teacher announced. 'Please sit down!'

Kaali sat down wherever she was standing.

'The place you chose today will be your seat for the rest of the year. The person on your right is your study partner.'

She turned nervously to see who her partner would be.

'No, child. That is left.' The teacher was looking at her.

Everyone started to giggle. She turned to her right. It was empty. *I suppose I will study alone. It is better than being poked and bullied. I'd rather study on my own*, she thought to herself.

～

School was not as fun as she had expected. It was difficult and exhausting. No one liked her there either. In fact, everyone actively hated her. She was tired of being called 'weird', 'pagal', 'mad', 'retard', 'fugly' and all sorts of names she'd given up keeping track of. She spent her time in classes alone. She spent her breaks alone. Each day during roll call everyone laughed at her name. No one wanted to be seen near her. She hated her school, but she hated home more. Days turned to weeks turned to months.

She found a quiet corner at school. She noticed no one liked to go there. It was away from the pond, and it did not have any delicious worms. So, she'd often spend her break time there. One day, she was sitting there watching the other ducks play when she thought to herself: *This isn't working out. If I have to stay in school for a few years, I have to make sure no one bullies me. Mother is right. Education is the only way I can make it in this world. This is the only way I can be seen and loved. I cannot miss out on this opportunity. So what should I do to make sure I am not shunned away? I have to be like them. If I cannot make it, I will fake it.*

She took out her notebook and pencil and started making a note of the different personalities in her class.

*Which of them can I imitate? That is the athlete. She is always in the field. Ugghh, it requires too much energy. That is the funny one—everyone laughs at what she says. That is too much attention. That is the attractive one whom everyone wants to date. That is a near-impossible goal to achieve considering how I look. These are the …*

Before she could complete her thought, she noticed a group of ducks coming closer towards her. She was so immersed in her thoughts that she did not notice them till she was surrounded. *These are the bullies, they always surround other ducks and make fun of them*, she completed her thought. There was no way she could escape. Not today.

'Oh, look at the Ugly Duckling,' one said.

'Why is she sitting alone?' asked another.

'Of course she's alone. Who wants to be friends with her?' a third duck said.

'Do you know, once, a cousin of mine befriended an ugly duckling, and she became ugly too!'

Her heart rate started to increase. She felt a tightness in her chest. 'Breathe in, breathe out, ten-nine-eight-seven-six-five-four-three-two-one...' They came closer and closer. Then suddenly, out of the blue, they started to punch her.

She was convinced they would beat her black and blue, but fortunately, they heard the voice of a teacher and quickly dispersed. The place was quiet again. Things were calm around her. Yet, she could hear her heart beat loud and fast. She was unable to breathe. She started flapping her wings. Repeated movement was her way to cope with fear. *Mother would get so angry if she ever saw me doing this*, she thought to herself. *The teachers would hate it too.* She hid there all day until school got over.

She was about to go home when she abruptly stopped. 'My schoolmates hate me, my parents hate me, my siblings hate me. Maybe I should run away.'

~

Feeling dejected, the duckling walked towards the lake that was her first home. She was lonely, and nostalgic. It had rained all day, just like the day she was born. A big rainbow covered the sky like a warm cosy blanket. The sky was a vibrant mix of red, orange, yellow and pink.

*All the other ducks will be on their way home after swimming all day*, she thought to herself. *If I go now, I will not have to face anyone. I can enjoy the lake to myself. I may even swim if I have the energy.*

When she reached the lake, it was empty. She sat there and watched the sun play hide-and-seek with the clouds. She watched the clouds change into fun shapes. She lost track of time. The sun started to set.

'Oh, how long have I been here?' she said to herself.

'It must have been at least two hours. I should find food and a place to sleep. I don't want to be found by the other ducks.'

The thought made her shudder with fear. So she quickly got up to leave when she saw an unbelievable sight. It was a flock of the most beautiful birds. She watched them with her beak wide open as they descended on the other side of the lake, diagonally opposite where she was standing. *Who are they?* she wondered.

On the one hand, she was scared to get closer. *What if they attack me like everyone else?*

On the other hand, she was really curious and wanted to get a closer look at them. Her heart was racing with excitement. *I will just take a sneak peek—only for research purposes. They won't even know I am there. They are probably too tired and thirsty.*

She tiptoed in their direction while continuously saying encouraging words to herself on loop.

'It will be fine. They will not attack you. They will not even know you are there. Ten-nine-eight-seven-six-five-four-three-two-one…'

She inched closer to where the group was perched. Hidden behind large trees, the sight ahead of her was nothing short of breathtaking. They were a flock of about twenty birds. They were jet black. Even though they looked tired, their feathers glistened under the sunset sky. Five of them were swimming in the lake. *They are swimming so smoothly. Almost as if they are floating on the water!*

Some others were resting on the banks of the lake. What struck her the most was how everyone was doing their own thing, yet managed to be mindful of each other's safety. Even though it was a large group, it was quiet and peaceful. Two or three adult birds were looking for food, and a group of children were swimming. She noticed one bird hiding under a bush, while another was peacefully sitting and flapping.

*I wish I had friends like them. I wish my family was like them. I suppose I should go back home. They hate me there, but at least I would be safe.*

Just as she was about to get up and leave, she saw one of the birds standing behind her.

'Who are you? I have not seen you in our flock before. Where is your flock?'

'I do not have one.'

'You don't have a flock?'

'No.'

'You are alone?'

'Sort of.'

'What sort of young bird moves around in a strange place? Why were you watching us?'

'I am sorry, I shouldn't have. I will leave now.'

'Leave and go where?'

'I don't know.'

'A young bird who is alone wants to leave but does not know where to go? That does not sound like a good idea.'

There was what seemed like a long pause. *What was I thinking? Is she going to attack me? Is she about to call her friends to bully me?* Her thoughts began to spiral. *Ten-nine-eight-seven-six-five-four-three-two-one... Ten-nine-eight-seven-six-five-four-three-two-one...*

'Sorry I forgot to introduce myself. My mother always scolds me for my lack of "social skills". According to rules, I am supposed to introduce myself. Do you have any idea who wrote these stupid rules? Anyway, I am Rekha, and you are?'

'I ...'

'You do have a name, right?'

'Yes …'

'And it is?'

'I …'

'Seriously girl, how can you forget your name?'

'I have not. I just don't like my name.'

'What is it?'

She sighed. *Why is this girl so relentless? Will she ever give up and let me leave?* She looked away from her and yet felt so drawn towards her. There was an odd sense of kinship that she could not explain.

'It is Kaali.'

'Really? Kaali? Which genius came up with that name?'

'I told you I do not like my name. I really hate it.'

'Sorry, I shouldn't have said that. I have a tendency to speak my thoughts out loud, especially when I am too tired. It is fine when I do that with my flock but outsiders often get very angry.'

'No, it is okay. I am like that too. Besides, I feel the same way about my name.'

'Fine. I will give you a new name.'

'What?'

'I will give you a new name. I have named all the young ones who were born after me. They say I am a natural.'

'I don't …'

'Yes. I once met this lovely girl during our journey.' The other bird's voice seemed to fade away, and she looked far away as if she could see that 'girl'. 'She was as beautiful as you.'

'I … What?'

'Her name was Rakhi. Do you like the name Rakhi?'

'Any name is better than Kaali.'

Rekha seemed to suddenly snap out of her reverie. 'Great. Your name is Rakhi. Now come with me.'

'Where are we …'

Before she could finish her sentence, Rekha announced loudly:

'Mother, Father look who I found here. She is my new friend. Her name is Rakhi. She lives alone. Can she please-please-please-please join us?'

'Well, honey, last time we met a *Rakhi* you pretended that she did not have a family either. Her parents almost filed a kidnapping charge against us.'

'This time it is the truth. Go on, ask her.'

The mother bird stepped forward to take a look at *Rakhi*. She expected the mother bird to belittle her, ridicule her, and shoo her away. Like her own mother. She stepped back and almost as if on instinct, tried to make herself smaller and smaller.

'Oh, the poor thing looks scared. Did you scare her with your questions again, Rekha?'

'I. Did. Not.'

'Yeah right. Now come in here. Are you hungry?'

'I ...'

'Do you want food? We have a lot because someone decided to bring in food for the whole neighbourhood.' She laughed, looking at Rekha's father.

'Here, I hope you like it. Rekha only eats not-mushy worms so we only collect those.'

Realizing that she did not have any way out, she ate. She was famished. She had not eaten anything all day. The food made her feel better.

'Do you want more?'

'No, thank you, ma'am.'

'Now, what is this business about not having a flock. Is it true?'

She looked down. Tears rolled down her face.

'Now, now. Don't cry. You are more than welcome to join us.'

'Really?'

'Yes please. I insist. It is not safe to be alone. A flock always helps. We will have to introduce you to everyone. Our flock does not like surprises so we are always careful about keeping everyone informed. We will also update our registry with your name.'

Turning to her daughter, she said, 'Rekha, go around and make sure you introduce her to everyone. We do not want others to get shocked when Rakhi joins us in our journey. After you are done, come back here and we will complete the paperwork for the registry.'

She accompanied Rekha.

'It is really quiet in here, isn't it?' Rakhi asked Rekha.

'Yes, we like it this way. Too much noise is stressful. If anyone wants to talk loudly or fight, we go to this place we call The Talking Corner. No one is allowed to talk loudly outside that area.'

Rakhi was already loving this flock. As she was being introduced to others, everyone oooh and ahhhed about how beautiful she was.

'Look at those feathers.'

'Look at her eyes.'

'Look at that smile.'

She was so confused.

'What is happening?' she kept muttering. 'Ten-nine-eight-seven-six-five-four-three-two-one ... Ten-nine-eight-seven-six-five-four-three-two-one ...'

After the paperwork Rekha asked, 'Care for a swim? Some of us are playing there. Do you want to join us?'

'Uh sure.'

No one had ever asked her to join a game. She walked to the lake with Rekha. A lake she was very familiar with. The water she was acquainted with. Yet, it felt different. As she was about to enter the lake, she suddenly stepped back.

'What happened?' Rekha asked.

She stood there silently. She looked at the water, and then at the flock. She looked back at the water, then back at the flock.

'Who is the bully in the group, Rekha? I want to avoid them.'

'What? No. We have a strict no-bully policy.'

'Okay! Who is the one who suddenly dives and stuff?'

'Why would anyone suddenly dive?' Rekha visibly shuddered.

'I don't know. There are some birds who do that and I get scared.'

'You get scared because it is scary. Why would anyone do that?'

'I don't know ...' She sighed.

'Okay, let's swim now.'

Rakhi took a step forward and paused again.

'Okay. You are making me nervous. I am the one who makes others nervous. What is happening?' Rekha said.

'You all look alike.'

'Yes, Sherlock. We are from the same flock.'

'All of you look alike,' she repeated.

'Yes, we do. Are you okay? Do you need glasses? Should I take you to the doctor?'

She was not listening to Rekha. 'All of you look alike. And I look like you?'

'Okay that's it. I am taking you to the doctor.'

'Rekha?'

'Yes?'

'What are you?'

'Huh?'

'What are you?'

'We are Swans.'

'Rekha?'

'WHAT?'

'What am I?'

'You are a Swan. I am a Swan. They are all Swans. Can we now please go swim?'

'Yeah, okay.'

Rekha dove into the lake. Rakhi paused.

'Rekha is a Swan. They are all Swans. I am a Swan. Rekha is a Swan. They are all Swans. I am a Swan. Rekha is a Swan. They are all

Swans. I am a Swan. I am not a Duck. I am not Ugly. I am a Swan. I am not a Duck. I am not Ugly. I am a Swan. I am not a Duck. I am not Ugly. I am a Swan. Rekha is a Swan. They are all Swans. I am a Swan.'

Her eyes met Rekha's. She smiled and dove into the lake. Rakhi felt something she had never felt before. She felt love. She felt acceptance. She felt seen and heard. All this while she had tried to belong somewhere. All this while she had tried so hard to be a perfect Duck. But in reality, she was already perfect. She was a Perfect Swan. This was where she belonged.

# Rapunzel and the People of Companara

*by Soumita Basu*

ONCE UPON A TIME, NOT SO LONG AGO, THERE WAS A beautiful province named Companara. It was covered with various shades of green—that is, if you saw it like our bird, Jack, from the top. Jack's favourite place in the whole province was the beautiful garden in the far-east corner. All of Jack's friends, like the shy sparrow and the singer parrot, also loved the garden. Every evening, all the birds congregated there and took their preferred seats on different trees. The black cuckoo's favourite was the mango tree, which was opposite Rapunzel's most colourful window. Every morning, the birds would sing their dearest Rapunzel's favourite song to wake her up. On spring evenings, however, the bird choir enjoyed listening to Rapunzel sing.

Rapunzel lived in the tallest tower in Companara. She could see the entire province when she looked out of her room. Her beautiful round room had big windows opening in all directions. They had beautifully carved frames and tinted glass in pink, green, yellow and blue. She could see the carpenters' village on the right side of the tower. On the left was the colourful village of potters. She could not see beyond those two villages, but every spring and fall, the bright kites from faraway rooftops made her curious.

Right in front was a dense forest with many wild animals; the tower was connected to the beautiful pink house beside it through an underground tunnel. That is where Mama Lovington lived. The beautiful garden surrounding the tower was a result of Mama Lovington's hard work of over forty-five years. The area used to be completely barren at the time Mama Lovington first took shelter here after she escaped. She slowly started planting her favourite fruits and vegetables. In a few years, it was the most beautiful garden in the province. You could smell the beautiful fruits and the intoxicating flowers even three villages away. No wonder this garden was Jack and his friends' favourite place. In fact, they liked it much more than the dense forest.

Every morning and evening, Mama Lovington brought the tastiest food in the province to Rapunzel in her handcrafted basket. Rapunzel would eagerly wait for the freshly baked buns that Mama Lovington made twice a week. On those days, Mama Lovington would climb up the long stairs of the tower to feed Rapunzel. It was an absolute joy for the old lady to see Rapunzel relish those buns with some homemade butter. But it was difficult for her old knees to climb the long staircase every day to go all the way up. That's why, on most days, she would stand under the window and call out, 'Rapunzel Rapunzel! Let it down.' Immediately, a thick, black silk rope would come down from the window. If you saw it, you would think it was a beautifully braided long stretch of hair. Mama Lovington would tie the basket at the end of the black silk rope and Rapunzel would swiftly pull it up.

Most of Rapunzel's days were spent chatting with her constant companion, Jack, the most colourful bird in the province. Actually, Jack was the most colourful bird in the entire region, with red and blue feathers nestling against his little tummy. Jack would often collect flowers from trees far and wide with his white beak that had black lines on it, and present them to Rapunzel. He even sat through the Zumba classes Rapunzel did with her monkey friends. Macnamara was the tallest monkey in the group. He was slow to move but he brought gifts for her, which always made her smile. He would pick up various pretty things from the villages when nobody looked. Once, he brought her an unusually coloured stone, tied with a little lace he had found at the tailor's window. (The tailor had so many that Macnamara was sure he would not miss a small piece!) Rapunzel kept it on her table, just beside the basket he had once brought her. Macnamara also told her stories about the people from whom he'd brought these gifts.

Books made Rapunzel the happiest. She loved reading while sunbathing on the terrace and often read herself to sleep. Most of the books were gifts from her parents, who brought them when they came to visit her. Both of them would travel for long periods outside the province. Rapunzel learned a lot about the world from their letters to her. They visited at least four times a year. Sometimes, they would visit more often if they missed their little girl more than usual. They brought her books on history, on people's lives, on experiments involving physics and chemistry, on gardening, biology and different cultures. Autobiographies were her favourite. Oh, and the travel books! She travelled far and wide with her books, all the while sitting on her terrace. And she grew wiser in the company of all the wise people across the world.

Jack also told Rapunzel stories from the neighbouring villages, and would often read out the Bird's Evening News Bulletin to her.

The parrot, Singer Somre, even made up songs about village life and added them to the bulletin.

Some days, Rapunzel really wanted to see all the villages of the province. With teary eyes, she would ask Mama L, 'Why must I stay in this tower all the time?'

And Mama L would shout back, 'How many times do I have to tell you! The world is a very bad place. Just stay here and be quiet.' This was the only time she would shout at Rapunzel.

Rapunzel was confused and would sometimes say in a low voice, 'But is it really so bad? Sometimes I see all these beautiful kites that people fly down there.'

'Why don't you ever listen to me? The world is much worse than you think. You must stay in this tower. I say this for your own good.'

These were the only times when Mama L would get upset with Rapunzel. Every time she got upset with her, she would bake fresh buns and make Rapunzel's favourite carrot cake. But she never ever allowed Rapunzel to meet anybody from outside. You see, Rapunzel was the apple of her eye, her only friend in the province, Amby's little daughter. Both Rapunzel's parents were doctors. Companara had always been known for good doctors, and people from neighbouring provinces would come there seeking treatments for difficult illnesses. But it was not easy for little children and old people who were very sick to travel much. So Rapunzel's parents would go to treat these children and old grannies and grandpas in other provinces for a few months every year. They also taught young doctors in other provinces about new ways of treating patients.

Rapunzel's favourite months of the year were when her parents stayed with her and told her stories of their travels. There were so many amazing people and beautiful things that could only be found in special places! Her favourite story was about a girl who didn't have legs but went to different places swimming in the rivers and oceans. Grandpa Tebog's story made her laugh the most. She always asked her father to repeat that story. Grandpa Tebog lived five provinces away and was completely blind. Whenever he stood at a corner of a road, people would just take his hand and help him cross the road. But they would never ask if he wanted to go! So, Grandpa Tebog kept going everywhere even when he just wanted to stand in a corner and enjoy the breeze. Rapunzel giggled and giggled imagining the plight of Grandpa Tebog. 'Oh! But why can't people just ask?' she would wonder, laughing. Jack and Macnamara found it amusing too. They always asked others, including Rapunzel, if they needed anything before trying to help them.

~

One evening, after the birds had gone to sleep, Rapunzel was looking out at the beautiful starry night, when she suddenly heard a strange noise. It sounded like somebody running fast but she couldn't see anyone. It was dark. The sound became louder and louder. The hissing of the wind was interrupted by the loud thuds of the runner. A strong smell started filling the air.

The young man was running as fast as he could to save his life. He was lost in the wild jungle. It was too dark for him to find his way back. The moment he saw the yellow light shining in Rapunzel's room, he started running in that direction. Every time he turned back, he could see a pair of green buttons shining in the darkness. The green buttons were coming closer and closer. He couldn't see anything else, only the shining green buttons. And the strong smell, which made his heart beat faster and faster. Soon he reached the fence of Mama L's garden.

Rapunzel could only see a few shining jewels running towards the garden and a pair of green shining buttons chasing them. She heard the young man call out, 'Help! Help!'

'Who are you? I can't see you.'

'I am Prince Haloux,' called the young man, as he climbed the fence.

Mama L had a very short fence. The villagers around were afraid to come anywhere near her, so the fence was only there to keep the animals away. Prince Haloux ran straight towards Rapunzel's window.

'Please tell me how to climb up! There are wild animals chasing me.'

A beautiful black silk rope suddenly appeared before the prince.

'Climb up! Quickly! The wild animals are coming closer,' she said.

'I am too tired! I have been running for hours!' the prince gasped as he struggled to climb.

'Tie the rope around your waist tightly. I will pull you up,' Rapunzel said as she saw the two green shining buttons grow larger. The prince couldn't believe that Rapunzel could pull him up the tall tower. But he was tired and scared, so he did as she said. She swiftly pulled him up and saved his life.

The wild bears with the green shining eyes rampaged through the garden to reach the prince. But Rapunzel had already pulled him up to safety.

The prince tumbled inside the room through the window. The moment he saw Rapunzel, he was mesmerized by her beauty. He bowed before her and took her hand to kiss it. 'Thank you for saving my life.' As he looked up again, Rapunzel could see his eyes filled with surprise.

'If you are a prince why were you alone in the forest? Where are your men?'

'I lost my way,' said the prince, and immediately blurted out in complete disbelief, 'how could you pull me up when you are in a wheelchair?'

'Well, I wheel myself all around the tower and also to the terrace, which has the best sunlight. Macnamara and my other monkey friends made a ramp from my room to the terrace. That's why my arms are very strong. I also pull Mama L up sometimes when she is really tired. I can't walk because of a defect in my legs. But I do have very strong arms.'

Prince Haloux had never met anyone like Rapunzel before. As they talked through the night, he could feel his heart beating faster with every word she said. Soon, it was dawn. He invited Rapunzel to his palace. Rapunzel's eyes shone at the prospect of seeing the province but she hesitated.

'Mama L will never allow me to go out. She says the world is a very bad place. She wouldn't even like me talking to you.'

'But the world is a beautiful place. You must come with me!'

'No, I can't. There is no ramp from the room to the garden.'

'We will find a way. I can carry you down.'

'Carry me? I don't think I would like that. I always go everywhere wheeling my own chair. Also, I can't go without Mama L's permission, and she always gets angry when I talk about going out.'

～

At the break of dawn, Mama L went for a walk in her garden like she did every day. She was shocked to see that much of it had been destroyed overnight. Fearing the worst, she ran up to Rapunzel's room in spite of her cracking knees. She immediately recognized the prince from his crown and the bejewelled belt that was shining as brightly as the wild bears' green eyes the previous night.

'How did you enter the tower?' she demanded.

'Mama, this is Prince Haloux. Wild bears were chasing him last night. I had to pull him up, like I pull you up sometimes, to save his life,' Rapunzel stepped in to explain excitedly.

'I want to invite you both to the palace as a mark of my gratitude,' said the prince, bowing to Mama.

'No!' shouted Mama L, 'I don't want to go anywhere.'

'I would be honoured if you accepted my invitation, just this once.'

'This world is a bad place. Please go back.'

'But, Mama, I have not met anyone and I don't have any friends from the villages apart from Jack and Macnamara,' said Rapunzel in a soft voice. 'Prince Haloux promised to show me the province. It has been my deepest desire. Mama, can we please...' she stopped when she saw tears roll down Mama L's eyes.

'No, no!' said Mama L through her tears. 'It's not your fault. Nobody comes to our house because they don't like me. That's why you don't have any friends. You know, my darling, how my skin bleeds sometimes and my face becomes full of blood drops? And the skin peels off from time to time because of my illness? I used to live just outside the potters' village. Every time people saw me, they would start screaming and run away. Children used to cry looking at the blood on my face. Their parents threw stones at me. Everywhere I went, people shouted "Witch, Witch!" ... that's why I keep telling you, it's a bad world out there!'

Rapunzel did not know that people were so cruel to Mama L because of her skin disease. This was the first time Mama L had shared her story. She gently hugged Mama L, stretching as much as she could from the wheelchair. Mama L continued, 'Amby is my dearest friend. She was the only one who didn't tease me or call me a witch. Your parents always took care of me when no one else did. When you were a little girl, you also had skin rashes. I was so scared that everyone would tease you too. Your parents were also worried about what people would say. People can say the harshest things without really understanding how they affect the other person. We decided to build this tower for you, so that you could get the best sunlight and fresh air from the garden. You were a little child, so the sun worked a special magic on you. Amby decided it was best if you stayed here. But people thought I had put a spell on you. When you couldn't walk anymore, villagers thought I did this to you. And after that, they would not come anywhere near my gardens. People really seem to think that I am a witch!'

The prince was saddened to hear this. He stepped forward, kissed Mama L's wrinkled hands and said, 'It is my duty as the prince of this province to make sure that you are treated well. Please come with me.'

By now, Jack and some of the other birds had joined them and heard the whole story. Jack sat on Mama L's shoulders and whispered, 'We will all take care of you. Rapunzel really wants to see the world. Let's make her dream come true.'

Mama Lovington agreed.

~

Everybody started planning how to bring Rapunzel down from the tower. They tied the wheelchair with the silk rope. All the monkeys formed a monkey chain and slowly pulled her down in the wheelchair as the prince gently let the rope down. The birds surrounded her to make sure she didn't fall. Mama L showed the prince the underground tunnel and soon, they were on their way to the palace.

Rapunzel cried out in pain when they started moving on the main road. The roads were so uneven that the wheelchair jerked heavily and hurt her back. She was finding it very difficult to wheel herself. There were steep slopes in places. Macnamara tried his best to make sure that she didn't fall. The prince tried to push the wheelchair from behind. Jack was on Mama L's shoulder and pecked her cheeks every time her eyes filled with tears.

After some time, Rapunzel was too tired to go on. 'I don't want to go any further. These roads are hurting me.'

The prince came forward. 'Please let me carry you. It will be my pleasure.'

'No, I don't want to be carried,' she cried, looking at him disappointedly. 'If the roads were better, I would have wheeled myself.'

'Don't worry, I will not hurt you. I will never let you fall.'

'But I don't want to be carried. I don't like being carried,' she struggled to explain. 'That's why they made a ramp from my room to the roof. I feel uncomfortable when people carry me. I like to carry myself! And I would do it too, if only these roads were not so bad! Being carried is not the safest thing. I really don't like it. Mama L never makes me do what I don't like. She always says I should only do something if it makes me happy. That I should not "adjust" and feel sad. Macnamara tells me the same thing then.'

'Will you not come to my palace?'

'Not till there are better roads for me.'

'I will make better roads for you! You see, you are the only person I know in a wheelchair in this province. Nobody else needed it before.'

Jack sighed and shook his head.

'Let me go back to my tower. If better roads are made, I will definitely come to your palace.' Saying this, Rapunzel turned back and struggled her way to the tower with the help of Mama L, Jack and Macnamara. A teardrop ran down Rapunzel's cheek. Jack slowly wiped it with his wings. He hugged her and held her as she said, 'Earlier, I used to spend all my time in this room and on the terrace. Sometimes I would feel sad that Mama L never let me go out, but all of you played with me and we would have so much fun. Macnamara and the other monkeys made me so happy when they built the ramp to the terrace. But today, when I finally went out to see the world,

I felt that nobody really wanted me. Those standing on the sides of the stPritis did not even remove the stones in the way, or even come forward to meet me.' That night she wept for hours.

Jack had noticed how sad the prince looked, too. He and the parrot went to meet the prince the next morning. The prince was delighted to see them.

'We can help you make a wheelchair-friendly province,' they said.

'Let's start right away then. Let me call the Chief Province Planner. The two of you can be our special advisors.'

Soon, the plans were ready. Prince Haloux called the best workers from the neighbouring provinces to finish the work quickly. They started working on making the palace completely disability friendly. Then the prince developed a blueprint with the Chief Province Planner to make the entire province wheelchair-friendly too, so that Rapunzel could come to the palace without suffering pain or hurting her dignity and independence.

Rapunzel did not expect the prince to return. She felt sad and sometimes even doubted herself; had she done the right thing? Should she have let the prince carry her just once even though she didn't like it? Did she lose her chance to be happy with the handsome prince? She sometimes hid her face away from Macnamara and Jack when these thoughts made her very sad. But they knew their dear Rapunzel's heart. They wanted her to be happy, but without feeling forced to do things she was not comfortable with, like being carried. They knew how being carried could be offensive. That's why they went to meet the prince every day and guided every step of making the province easy for everyone to navigate. They remembered Grandpa Tebog, and put up a sign on the stPriti corners: 'Ask before you help'. The prince didn't understand the meaning of this but he let them continue. They kept all this a secret from Rapunzel. They wanted to surprise her.

~

And indeed, she was very surprised! Rapunzel could not believe her eyes when she saw the prince at her window again. He had also brought a special vehicle that could go all the way up to Rapunzel's window. The vehicle had a very long crane that could be moved to settle against any place, turning it into a very long ladder.

'May I please invite you to my palace? All the roads are now easy to wheel on. And my palace also has ramps.'

Rapunzel danced and twirled in her wheelchair with excitement. She moved the wheels onto the special crane that brought her down into the garden. Her heart started beating faster and faster as she approached the main road. She recalled how painful it was. But this time, she moved easily on the smoothly paved road. All the stones had been removed and the slopes were now flatter. Her eyes widened as she went through the villages that she had only seen from the tower. She smiled at everyone that she passed.

She had never seen so many people before. It was a little overwhelming at first. With everyone talking to each other and going about their daily lives, there were so many sounds that Rapunzel had never heard before. At one corner, she heard a soft swirling around, just a little movement of air. Turning the corner, she saw a huge potter's wheel. That's where the sound was coming from, with every turn the wheel took! She had seen it so many times from the tower, but to see it so close, hearing it with each move, seeing the smaller lines on the wheel move in synchronized way … it was all so new! As she moved ahead, she saw the peels of wood spewing every time the carpenter shaped things. He was wearing a red cap that Rapunzel immediately recognized. From the rooftop she could see many people working their doors and wooden frames, but this carpenter always wore a red cap. It was the first time she was seeing his face—and the first time he was seeing hers.

Mama L walked beside Rapunzel, worriedly looking around as she passed by her old village. People were surprised to see her, but no one dared to call her a witch or throw stones when they saw the prince with her. Some of them were scared too, but when they saw the prince walking so close by and smiling at Mama L, they felt more comfortable. Rapunzel burst into the most melodious laughter the prince had ever heard when she saw the signs Jack and Macnamara had put up in the stPriti corners. Rapunzel told the prince the story of Grandpa Tebog. The prince laughed too as he now understood the meaning of 'Ask before you help'.

Closer to the palace, the prince was surprised to see a few children on wheelchairs playing together. He didn't know there were other wheelchair users in his province.

He was even more surprised when he saw many people on wheelchairs join the National Day celebrations at the palace ground the following week. Rapunzel was his special guest, and as a surprise, her parents were also invited as royal guests. The invitation was personally delivered by Jack! Rapunzel had been hoping to see them soon, but she wasn't expecting them for another few months because they were on a long medical trip. So it was truly a great surprise. They were really proud of their daughter. Rapunzel had told them about the prince in her letters. But it was from Mama L's letters that they understood how their daughter had not succumbed to 'adjusting', but instead was the reason that Prince Haloux had made an inclusive space for everyone in the whole province!

They were given special seats in the front row and Rapunzel was beside Prince Haloux when the king hoisted the flag. The king delivered a special speech about Rapunzel and how she had helped the province of Companara be a better place. For the first time, the king talked about illnesses in his official speech to the people. He explained about skin rashes and bleeding too. Drops of tears rolled down Mama L's face. For the first time she felt comfortable being around so many people. She could now hope that people would not misunderstand her and her illness.

To Prince Haloux's surprise, there were three new musicians on wheelchairs who had joined the Royal Orchestra. He looked at Rapunzel and said, 'I didn't know there were so many people on wheelchairs in this province.'

Rapunzel smiled. 'That's because there were no good roads.'

# It's Still Your Choice

## *by Nidhi Ashok Goyal*

HI, MY NAME IS ADITI.

And I am twenty-one years old. Actually, twenty-one years young will be the more appropriate description. I recently turned twenty-one, on 21 November. Yeah so, this year I guess twenty-one is my favourite number. Ah well, this year and all other years since you know I love me and me was born on twenty-one.

I live in Mumbai, and I have recently completed my bachelor's in commerce. Did I like it? Na, just did it, was too confused after the accident. The accident in which I lost my sight.

I had a month to decide during my recovery, and I had heard that all blind folk end up taking arts, and that is the easiest to do, so I basically went against the tide, and said, 'Well, I have a month to decide, and I will decide to go against the tide.' After I met with the accident, I was literally crumbling from the inside. I had a lot to be grateful for in my life later, but not the experience of that accident, the pain, the anguish, the darkness. That I lived through when I was fifteen.

Who was I before the accident? A chatty kid, a moody teenager, a short girl fascinated with high heels, and certainly someone with heaps of dreams. Well, I forgot the most important thing, I guess: I was the apple of my papa's eye and the adorable troublemaker of my mamma's home. My parents were often asked why they decided to have only me and not another child. They would laugh and say, 'She is the boy and the girl, the whole package for us. She keeps us busy and is a handful.' Maybe Mum said this in relation to the foot I fractured at six while trying to pluck a mango without any experience in climbing trees. Or maybe she was talking about the time I cut her saree into pieces when I was nine because I wanted a certain pattern for my dress, or the time I was twelve when I pretended to be my papa's PA and tried to fix up an appointment. You get the gist …

And, of course, I remember how I continued 'to be a handful' even after the accident. I kept their hands full of medical reports, of hospital bills, of anxious nights, days of teenage tantrums and many more things I was not exactly proud of. But they were determined to walk with me through, literally and figuratively, the darkest patch of my life. If that meant that they had to hold my hand and teach me once again to walk, they did—only with a white cane this time; if that meant that they had to help me read and write again, they did—by taking me to training centres for screen reader learning; if that meant that they had to encourage me again in the toddler phase of my blindness to learn to meet people and forge connections again, they did—this time by ensuring that I was not left out of any gatherings or events.

But let us not spend time dwelling in dark memories. For me, life has been beautiful. I have my lovely parents, my self-confidence, my degree in French, and umm yes, my prince charming. French, I was told, was the language of love, and it was French that helped me find my love. I think my angel or fairy godmother must have whispered to me to get myself registered for French classes at French-Wiz. This was a new-age fairy godmother who gave me ideas based on her intuition, and told me dreams or fantasies only came true if you worked for them. And so, with trepidation but also excitement, I registered for a language class, and not just to cut the boredom of economics and commerce, but also to perhaps learn the beautiful, much-fantasised-about language of love. I had no idea that it would be the beginning of my Cinderella story. I had begun to suspect in dark moments that these tales were not for me, a disabled girl.

My first day, I was eighteen and had no idea if I would fit in the class, if the teachers would be trained enough to support me in learning French, or if they'd be hostile. If they were hostile, it would not be my first experience, and I told myself it would probably not be the last. I remember I had kissed my papa and received one of the rare hugs from my mamma while I was leaving home, and I believed that their love would see me through this next milestone, like it had helped me with all the others.

The rainy day did not help my speed or the traffic on the way. I had to change three modes of transport, autorickshaw, metro and autorickshaw again. Gosh, I could not reach the class like a drowned mouse. I was not wearing my heels—I preferred not to in Mumbai monsoons, what with my precarious balance, which had nothing to do with my blindness. First impressions were important to me, and I had dressed carefully as always. Jeans, monsoon footwear, black knitted t-shirt, a chain with the pendant dangling just near my breastbone, a few oxidised bracelets stacked on my right wrist and a metallic watch on my left wrist, and a light fragrance.

I reached the building reception nervously. 'I am here for my French class, beginners' batch please.' I extended my class enrollment receipt. Without a word, the receptionist took the receipt from my hand—a disappointing start. But then, I soon heard the phone clicking and a female-sounding voice saying, 'Hello that student is here. *Arre baba*, the student who has a problem no ...'

I was not surprised; people often referred to me as someone with 'a problem', and I often feel like responding that the only problem I have just now is you and your ignorance. But I kept shut. 'Aree,' she continued whispering, 'she has this vision thing no baba, that student.'

'You can tell them that Aditi Arora is here for the beginners' batch, and she lives with blindness,' I had to jump in. I heard the receptionist pause and then clear her throat before I heard the phone click.

'Please wait,' is all that she said, perhaps taken aback by my interruption, or uncomfortable with the word 'blindness'. At the end of ten minutes, I was beginning to get annoyed when I heard a deep masculine voice approach me and say, 'Aditi, hi, I am Krish. Welcome to French-Wiz.'

All I could think of in that moment was melting chocolate, warm honey and the smell of the ocean—his voice brought the combination of all of this within its rich tone.

Before I could lose my teenage-hormone-filled mind, I said, 'Hey Krish, pleasure to meet you.' Saying this I extended my hand and eagerly waited this time for the touch, which didn't come.

'I teach the advanced French batch here, and we teaching staff thought it would be good for me to support your orientation.' He had not offered to shake hands and was being quite rude, but why? Maybe my instant attraction was showing on my face. Straightening up and pulling my hand back, I said a little less graciously, 'Sure, thank you.'

'Great, welcome to the French journey. I am extending my hand.' I felt childish and for a moment I did not want to shake hands, but my curiosity won. The delay at my end was enough; he snapped his fingers and said, 'Here is my hand.'

Oh shit, he was blind too. The realization dawned on me and why he had not shaken hands when I offered became clear! As I shook his hand and took his elbow so he could assist me in the orientation, I sheepishly smiled and berated myself on falling prey to a typically non-disabled behaviour. This is what people did to me, extended hands without saying anything, and I had done the same. But I could not think about disability or anything else too much as his musk, a woody perfume, surrounded my senses and his muscles flexed below my hand while we continued our walk to my French class and other beginnings.

The first day was a blur—the effort to introduce myself to other students, gauging the route and structure of the class, and paying attention to many new words and the syllabus. I was, as usual, carrying my digital recorder, to record lessons while I was taking notes, so that I could ensure that I did not miss important pieces from the lecture. And all that time, I was aware of one voice, one perfume, which stood there to assist me in Rose Madam's class, just the way he assisted me, holding my hand and guiding me respectfully.

It was Friday, and almost a week had passed. I had not seen Krish after the first day, but I knew he was there, and once I had a handle on French, I would surely seek him out, or maybe not. I wanted to stop dreaming and start working. Pulling out my laptop, I started going through my notes and class work for the week. I started reciting the alphabet and numbers. Wait a minute, I thought. I was pronouncing a few numbers differently from Rose Madam. Hmm, I would have to go through the recorder. I slipped my hand into my laptop bag to where I stored my recorder and, oops, it was not there. This was followed by a frantic search, by the end of which I'd turned the bag almost inside out. *Shit shit double shit.* Where was my recorder? It was not just about the notes; I had this annoying habit of sometimes treating the recorder as my personal diary when

I was too lazy to write entries on my laptop and it had some pretty personal stuff. How could I be so stupid? When had I lost it, and where? Think, Aditi, think. I slammed the heel of my hand on my head. My cell phone rang. *Uhh, I don't have time for unknown callers right now.* The ring was persistent.

'Hello,' I said in an agitated state.

'Hey, Aditi,' the voice arrested my agitation. *This could not be … am I hallucinating? Did I think of him too much?* 'Is this Aditi?' the voice repeated.

'Yes, may I know who this is?' I asked despite having a very good idea.

'This is Krish from French-Wiz. You have forgotten your recorder here. A staff brought it to me since mine was the last batch for the evening,' he said. I should have been relieved, except I was not. My recorder, my personal thoughts were in his hands! 'Aditi, you there?'

'Yes, Krish, ummm Krish Sir?'

He laughed and said, 'Please, no need for the formality, I am not teaching you directly, just call me Krish.'

I smiled and said, 'Okay then, Krish, how can I collect the recorder?'

'What do you mean?' he said in a somewhat puzzled voice. 'Can't you just take it on Monday when you come in for the next class?'

'No NO,' I responded emphatically. 'I mean, I might need to refer to it for my notes over the weekend, it is quite urgent. Can I come down to the institute and take it now?'

'Don't be silly,' he said. 'Don't make a trip all the way to the institute just for this.' Then he paused. 'Where do you live?'

'Goregaon West.'

'Then coming all the way to Andheri East does not make sense at all. I am planning to visit Inorbit Mall tomorrow. Would you like me to get it there and perhaps you can collect it from me?'

Was his pause restless, curious, anticipatory? Was this a date?

'Ah well, of course, if it is not too much trouble for you, I would certainly love to meet you at Inorbit. What time? Where?'

'The Italian cafe at 11 a.m. See you there.'

I hung up with a smile. I whooped with excitement and then immediately sobered up with the thought that he might just hear the personal reflections my recorder contained.

This called for a girl conference. I called Priti and Anju, and told them about my week, pouring out all my excitement and anxiety.

'Why would you not just use your phone to record stuff, Aditi?' sighed Priti, my girl pal from school.

'Because she is a peculiar one,' said Anju. 'Are you really nervous, Ads?' she asked.

I paused and heard my heart beating with the patter of the rain outside and said, 'Well, let's see tomorrow.'

They both chuckled and probably rolled their eyes as well, but they still sounded excited for me. Anju, in a contemplative voice, said, 'This will be great, he may be the man you were waiting for.' And there was something in her voice and tone—and the fact that she thought that a man would be right for me for the first time in my life—that reassured me. Considering the history of our conversations, I was almost sure she was saying this because Krish was also blind. 'He will surely fall for you,' she said. I was too happy to respond to innuendos or to unpack what she exactly meant, not through her words but through her tone. I covered my face with my blanket and went off to sleep.

At 11 a.m the next day, I was at the mall and on the escalator to reach the cafe. The mall security guard assisting me was very polite and respectful, except for the, 'Madam, let's go towards the lift please, escalator will be too dangerous.' While she was arguing with me, I stepped on to the escalator smoothly with my white cane. She was so worried that she didn't pay attention to where she was stepping, so she stumbled and had to balance quickly to stabilise herself.

After that, she silently and without protest took me to the second floor where Krish Khanna, the tall, gorgeous Krish Khanna with the sexy voice, was waiting for me. I reached the cafe, and the person at the reception immediately said, 'Madam, yes yes Sir is waiting for you.' And then he just grabbed my hand and led me to the table where Krish was sitting.

As I sat down, I asked him, 'Hey, had you told them you were waiting for me?'

He said, 'No, not really, just mentioned I was waiting for a friend.' That was probably not the best opening question and I now needed to explain the awkward opening.

'Sorry Krish, it just amuses me and annoys me a bit actually.'

In his patient teacher tone, he asked, 'What does?'

'That two blind folks would come to a restaurant to meet each other only not anyone else,' I said with a dash of exasperation.

'Well, I feel they thought a handsome young man and this beautiful young woman seem like they would have come here for each other and perhaps that is why they brought you straight to my table,' he said with a straight face but with mischief in his voice, and I didn't quite know if that was meant as a compliment, an attempt at flirtation or just a way to take my mind off the issue. But all the nervous anticipation kicked back into all my muscles and for a brief moment my pulse beat in my ear so hard that I almost missed his next words, 'Here you go, you seemed very anxious to have this back.' He extended his hand, holding the recorder almost to my side and nudged my palm facing down to take it. For a second, both of us were holding the recorder and in my nervous state I think I pressed the recorder too hard. Much to my chagrin, my voice emerged.

*'I just can't tell you how I feel, I have had crushes, instant attractions, but this time as he snapped his finger and I shook his hand, it felt like my fairy godmother, my guardian angel deliberately sent me to this institute so that I could meet him.'*

For an instant both of us were silenced by these words and our hands stilled on the recorder. Then I jerked it out of his hand and pushed all the buttons hard. By now my palms were sweating and I did not know where to look or what to do. The silence that followed was deep and charged, and I was not going to be the one that broke it.

'*So*, can we safely say that the shoe Cinderella left behind has now been returned by Prince Charming?' he inquired in his caramel chocolate voice. Very few situations could render me speechless, and this was one of those. It felt like electricity was charging through me, but at the same time, a full-body-bind spell was cast on me. I heard a gentle snap of the fingers and he said, 'Hey, Aditi, I am Krish, can I shake hands with you?'

While my heart did jumping jacks, I put on a confident and collected voice to say, 'With pleasure, Krish. With pleasure.'

And he did not leave that hand as we traversed the next chapter of our lives.

~

The journey grew richer through the years. Krish was half a decade older than me, a creature of habit which included his gym, his family time, his work in his family's textile business, and then his personal habits of chatting with his girlfriend and kissing his girlfriend. He radiated confidence, but over the years, I learnt that Krish had a serious and reserved personality. He was an astute observer and a silent conversationalist, practised in the art of punctuating discussions with witty remarks. I often felt amazed at how and where he'd got the cockiness to ask me out at the cafe. He'd mostly brush it off with a smile. Sometimes, he would say that my perfume intrigued him, sometimes my handshake and long fingers, and other times he would tease me and say that my flirtatious grip on his elbow had done the trick for him. But I know that in this world of LinkedIn, Instagram and X, he had known much about me before the day we actually met.

~

This week was extra special, not just because I had turned twenty-one a day ago, but my parents were off to a Vipassana centre, a meditation retreat where they had to cut off all connections and communications for seven days, and I had convinced them to let me be by myself at home. Of course, the fact that Anju and Priti were within walking distance helped my case and I was going to taste sweet freedom. Not like my parents had ever controlled me, or stopped me from doing anything, but as a young person, the sense of freedom that came from being unsupervised or rather in my case unobserved had a certain appeal. Plus, this was the week Nishi, Krish's sister, was going to get married, and I had promised to help them and join in on all the fun.

On the first day of being home alone, I got up bright and early and got dressed and dashed to his house. I had to take him for last-minute fittings, and this also meant that we would get some alone time. He had been grouchy this past week and it was important for me to spend time with him and give him the space to voice what was upsetting him.

Well, in his case it could just be the prospect of hundreds of people arriving in three days. Krish was not fond of large crowds and that was certainly not because he was blind. I mean, look at me, I was blind, and I loved being with people and interacting with them.

I reached his house and met his family, who I now knew very well: Pummy Aunty and Ram Uncle, Krish's parents, and of course Nishi—Krish's baby sister, just two years older than me.

He was moodily sitting on his work chair and all I wanted to do was to hug him tight. I stood behind the chair and hugged him from the back.

*Thud.* The bedroom door opened. 'Oh aunty, good morning,' I had known it was her from the sound of the fifteen-odd bangles she wore.

Unapologetic for opening the door without knocking, she asked, 'What are you kids doing?'

Very coolly I responded, 'I was showing Krish some of the screen reader shortcuts he did not know.' It was very easy sometimes to smoothly lie even in obvious situations, because our blindness gave us that cover. People (like Trisha and the person at the restaurant) either thought two blind people were made for each other, or that they weren't capable of any naughty behaviour (like Pummy Aunty!).

Ah well, Krish abruptly got up and said, 'Mom, we are heading out anyway.'

'Yes, yes.' Pummy Aunty waved her hands around Krish's room and said, 'Aditi, make sure he looks handsome and the fittings are good and get him some more dashing clothes. There are very special guests coming in tomorrow.' I felt Krish stiffen at these words. 'But Aditi beta, how will you both manage? Let me ask someone else to come with you.'

I did not want to lose my patience; Pummy Aunty was a contrast to my parents. 'Aunty, we will manage, don't worry—'

Before I could finish my statement, Krish was out of the house and I had to practically run to catch up with him. Rolling our white canes down his apartment building, we got into Krish's car and I gently directed the driver to the shop we had to first go to.

We shopped in silence. He just refused to share what was on his mind. After hours of silence, I asked, 'Is it meeting all these new people—are you nervous? Has someone said something? What is it, Krish?' He just hugged me and shook his head, but I knew he was fighting something inside him, and the battle was not easy. But on this happy occasion, what could this battle even be? *Oh my God, is Nishi okay, are they asking for dowry or something? Is everything okay with the marriage?* My mind was running a hundred miles every second and I was getting exhausted and anxious with the silence. 'Nothing, can we not discuss this today? Please,' he said, his voice so full of some emotion that I could not recognize or pinpoint. I gently stroked his hair and squeezed his hand. Maybe it was saying bye to his baby sister. Nishi was after all moving to Toronto, from where visits would be infrequent, and the chasm would be felt.

I barely managed to change when I got home that night. The day had been hot and humid and exhausting and Krish's silence was emotionally draining. I woke up with a start to my phone ringing ... *gosh what time was it?* 7.30 a.m. and Priti was calling.

'Hey, you never called yesterday after returning from Krish's.'

I yawned before responding, 'Sorry ya, I just fell asleep, was very tired. But I'll come home on time today—I have my beautician coming over in the evening. Need to sort out my face and hair, before the functions start tomorrow. Why don't you and Anju come over for dinner? We'll have a pizza night.'

'Done done, remember, don't look *too* gorgeous—you can't outshine the bride.'

Priti was always the positive light of my life, someone who kept me going and loved me immensely, my sister from another birth.

I added cornflakes to a bowl of milk and gulped it down cold before getting ready for the Khannas'. The guests were going to start trickling in and I was dressed appropriately: a long bandhani dress with a dupatta and a low back with a tie-up and tassels—Krish loved those. When I entered the Khanna house, I saw that some friends of the family from Punjab had come. Which also meant that I could not waltz into Krish's room, but had to sit with the others in the living room. In the first five minutes, it became apparent that they were a political family and had a daughter who had just turned eighteen. She had already been introduced to the kitchen and was expertly handling the tea and snacks and serving them to all of us. I tried to engage her in conversation.

Her name was Mehar, and was called 'gudiya' by most. Pummy Aunty seemed fond of her and, maybe I was wrong, but there was something in the way she called her 'beta'. I was beginning to get bored and Krish had not yet emerged from his room.

'Dude, where are you?' I texted him. 'This is truly boring. Trying to talk to your Punjabi relatives.'

As if on cue, Pummy Aunty turned to me and said, 'Aditi, why don't you and Mehar spend time with Krish in his room? When Nishi comes back from the parlour, I will send her along too.' *Finally! At last!* I exhaled, albeit not audibly, and started heading towards Krish's room. I didn't know Mehar and I didn't know how the conversation would go.

I knocked and waited for the muted reply. It was more muted than yesterday, and my irritation was immediately replaced with concern. 'Are you okay, Krish?' I asked as soon as I was inside the room. I thought his grunt was marvellously verbose. But I kept my comments to myself; after all, Mehar was in the room.

She shyly asked me, 'Can I ask you a question? How do you manage? You are dressed up so well, all is matching-matching also.'

I smiled and patiently started my informal education session on how I was passionate about dressing up and invested time and care in it and that applying lipstick or kajal was not a big deal.

She said rather boldly, 'Would you like to check out my earrings? They are similar to yours but longer.'

With her permission, I touched her earring. 'Very nice,' I said.

She promptly turned to Krish and said, 'Would you not want to see what I am wearing,' with such familiarity that I was taken aback for a minute. There was a brief silence, after which the door opened with a thud. Of course, Pummy Aunty.

'What are you kids doing?'

With a blush that seeped into her voice, Mehar responded, 'Nothing Aunty, just …'

Pummy Aunty took over, 'Krish you know how beautiful Mehar is? She has long hair and fair skin. She is five-eight, so tall like you, and is wearing a light pink suit with an intricately designed phulkari dupatta.' She paused and turned towards me. 'Aditi, isn't Mehar beautiful?'

*Umm.* Before I could respond, she went on to say, 'Arre ohho how will you know na, how beautiful she is. By the way, Aditi, Krish is also very handsome, tall and fair, actually now that I see both of them together, they—'

'Mom,' Krish cut in.

'Yes, Krish?' She innocently continued, 'Mehar's bangles are exquisite, look.' I heard Mehar's bangles move like someone was lifting her hand.

It was followed by Krish's agitated response, 'Mom, please.'

'Come on, Krish, tomorrow *toh* you have to hold this hand when you slip on the ring,' she said.

'Sorry whose hand, what ring?' I blurted out before I could stop myself. Krish said nothing.

It was Pummy Aunty who spoke again, 'Arre beta, for others we will announce directly at the function, but you are *toh* like family now, Krish's best friend, almost someone who could be his best man. He is getting engaged tomorrow.' Saying this, she exited the room.

I could hear everything and nothing; there was a buzzing in my ear and numbness in my hands. All I could say was 'Krish' and that single word was a plea, a command, a hope, a question. And I heard nothing. No response, just the squeaking of the rotating office chair which happened when Krish swung back and forth on it.

'Mehar, could you please get me a glass of water?'

She was more than happy to comply with Krish's request.

I repeated, 'Krish?' This time, there was an urgency in the question and a hopelessness.

'I have been asked to get engaged tomorrow. I've been wanting to tell you this for a few days now. There was nothing I could do.'

How did the seven colours of the rainbow turn grey? Was the sun setting in the afternoon? Was it possible to get paralysed just sitting down?

'Krish ...' The third time, that word was full of sadness, shock, disappointment.

Oblivious to the situation, Mehar entered with a glass of water, which, in her eagerness to give to her future fiancé, slipped. The breaking of the glass and the splashing of the water brought life back into my limbs, but I knew that life would perhaps never be back in my heart. Ever.

Silently I walked out of the house, not caring who thought what. But I could not make it farther than the park bench of the neighbourhood. I was not crying, I was not angry, I just felt like everything in me was dead. All I could think of was Papa and Mamma, and I couldn't speak to either one now. No one. Panic started building within me and just then Priti called, 'Hey I was checking in, wanted to see if you needed me to get anything for dinner—'

'Priti ...' The way I interjected spoke volumes. I would still not cry, I would not.

'Are you okay, Ads? What happened?'

'Priti, can you come get me, I don't think I can move.'

'What happened, Ads, just tell me, I am forty-five minutes away from you. Can you get up? Are you hurt? Where is Krish? Talk to me, please.'

'I am …' And the dam burst.

'I am calling Krish.' That got me out of my sobs.

'No, don't call him, never call him.'

There was a silence at the other end and an audible curse. 'I am booking a cab for you, get into it and I will see you at your house. Don't do anything stupid till then.'

No day had been so long. I alternated between sobs, which shook my body and soul, and silent paralysis. Inhalations and exhalations were becoming a task. The memory of the cold words—'I have been asked to get engaged tomorrow.'

Delivered with aloofness.

The shopping for special dresses kept hitting me like jets of fire. I was actually shopping for my boyfriend so that he could look handsome while getting engaged to another woman. Before I could stop, my fingers had typed the text: '*Why, Krish?*'

Call me foolish but I could not help but check my texts for a response constantly, and every time there were no new messages, my heart was punctured all over again. Priti and Anju were there. Was it evening already? They had walked into my room with me silently and seen the glittering dresses which I had laid out this morning, all ready to show them. But now these dresses were only adding insult to injury. Did they expect me to dress up and dance for his engagement? I broke down in their arms and their words were just a bunch of sounds. In between racking sobs, I told them the entire story. My hair was a mess, and my clip was just hanging in there, in my messy curls. My eyes were red. I felt like everything I had or had not eaten would come out of me.

'Listen to me, Aditi, he was clearly under pressure, but if he has succumbed to it, he is a coward, and it is not your fault. NOT YOUR FAULT, understand.'

I didn't respond, but I did not understand, I did not want to. I just wanted him back. Anju spoke more tentatively, 'Was this girl normal ...? I mean able-bodied? Then I sort of understand the mother's concern. But it was shitty of him not to tell you.'

'So, you think it is okay to dump me for a presumed "better" woman because she is just non-disabled, Anju?' This time was one too much. 'Is his only fault not telling me? What about the fact that he broke my heart, Anju?'

She was taken aback. I usually overlooked the not-so-subtle dismissals that I faced from her many times.

'I don't mean it that way; I understand you are heartbroken and that you're just lashing out at me.'

'Yes, I *am* heartbroken, but I am lashing out because of your thinking.'

Priti jumped in. 'We love you. We are here for you, Aditi.'

They managed to get me to nibble at my food at least, and cleared the kitchen before saying their goodbyes. I had refused Priti's offers to stay with me, because I knew I had a long night ahead of me. The silence, with no text from Krish, was smothering me. Making me lose life bit by bit. Was he ready to leave me for someone just because they had sight? Did he have a choice? Why did he not stand up for us? Had he ever believed in us and our future? There were many questions and a single answer—silence. For hours and hours I sat reliving the last words that Krish spoke to me. The words that felt like spikes were being run through my body. Flitting in and out of despair, I occasionally remembered to drink water and resisted all forms of food. I was missing Mamma and Papa. I wanted to hide in them again, be a little child who they could protect. The first time they had gone for Vipassana, I had lost my sight in the accident. This time, I lost my love and life.

Two days had passed and all that was left were buckets of silence that poured on me like lava of grief. The room represented my emotions. Clothes scattered everywhere like the chaos in my life, my unruly curls in a tangle and dark circles that narrated their own story. But it was only day four, another three days before I could reach my parents. I was frantically hoping for a miracle to have them back when it struck me. With impatient fingers, I pressed the start button on my laptop and started reading.

~

Diary entry:

*'Which one will you wear Aditi? There are two new dresses that you were gifted on Rakhi.' It was 7.45 p.m. and we had to leave for Papa's friend's housewarming at 8. My palms were clammy, my heart was galloping, and I was wondering if pretending to be unwell would help me get out of this one. As if my thoughts were on speakerphone, Mamma stroked my hair and said, 'No problem will find its own solution, beta.' Saying this, she laid the dresses on either side of my lap. 'Choose.'*

*And I started the exploration of the material, the work and the pattern. And the neckline that always fascinated me. I almost smiled to myself but withdrew hastily.*

*'Just choose, Mamma, it's not like I am going to know which one is looking better and how I am going to look in them.'*

*There was a minute of loaded silence, in which I imagine my mum was trying to reign in her emotions and her temper. In a wobbly voice but with a firm tone she said, 'You get to choose, and you will choose, because what you make of life will still be your choice. I want you dressed in five minutes, Aditi. I am waiting in the hall.'*

*Saying this, she almost turned away, but before her footsteps could retreat, she brushed her hand gently on mine and they spoke more than her words could.*

I sobbed harder and kept wiping my own tears while my other hand opened the other entry. I wanted to wipe out these words of wisdom, and another part of me wanted to hear my parents again, even if through my own diary memories. I needed them.

*They had finally discharged me, and I was sitting up in bed resting my head against the headrest. My curls were neatly tied back, because I was certainly not finding the pleasure of swirling them around my face and looking in the mirror at how they bounced near my dimples in the step cut. My face was passive, but my soul felt like it had been dipped in a boiling pot of bitter curry—the burn and bitterness both scalding me. Don't get me wrong, I was not going to harm myself or anything, but I really was not able to find the point of life or the meaning of it. And just then, my favourite person walked into the room. Yes, I did hear the footsteps, yes, I did smell his aftershave fragrance and the dip on the bed confirmed that Papa had come to speak to me. He did not ask me how I was or any other such question. He just started off with a story like he did when I was a baby. 'Let me tell you the story of when I was a child.' And he knew he would have my attention. I was going to hear about my superhero, and I could never turn away from that.*

*'I was a smart kid but the teachers had no idea and we were in a government school with very few amenities. Half the class was grade four and the rest was grades five and six combined. I was in grade four and the teacher suddenly realized that I was*

*responding to some of the questions intended for grade six. The teacher was curious, I was happy, and the older kids were jealous. In the break they wanted to bully the kid who could do things better than them ... they called me names. They reminded me big dreams are not good for poor kids and did everything to squash me. Finally, one of them pushed me and took the twenty paisa I had saved. I ran home. Not because I could not fight back, But I knew if I ignored them and did what I had to, I would eventually earn back the twenty paisa and much more, and of course their grudging respect. I was happy with the news and ran home also hoping that this news would mean the tea with sugar for a change for me. But I reached home and the atmosphere was worse than the day before. I only saw long faces and empty plates. Finally, in silence, we sat down to eat and relish the spicy water. We were sixteen of us and the household barely had more than 250 grams of a vegetable on an average day. So, what each of us got in the dona was very spicy water which had been brushed with the memory of a vegetable. There were many such days, but this day stuck with me because I talked to myself that day. A long chat that brought me to a crossroads—to see life in the bare realities that it was today, or to envision what life could be if I chose to keep going on. From that day, every day, I told myself that I was a part of an Olympics race—just jumping over the hurdles and my readiness to jump would leave each hurdle behind. Instead of anticipating more barriers, I said to myself one hurdle down and decided to taste victory with each step. In all this I didn't lose one thing, the thought of a dream, a vision of a different life.'*

At the end of the story, his voice was dry and mine was wet, both feeling the pain of each other from the past, in the present and of the future.

*'There is pain in falling or being pushed, and there is greater pain in standing up again, but one pain will pull you back and the other will take you ahead. You have to choose which one you embrace.'*

I wiped my tears and got out of bed. I knew I was just about managing to put one foot ahead of the other. But I knew one thing: that in six days, six weeks or six months, Cinderella will have to rewrite what happily ever after meant to her.

# Cinderella's Sister

## *by Somrita Urni Ganguly*

## 1.

WHY WAS THE PRINCE THE ONLY PERSON WHO could save her?

Sitting on Ma's lap, breathing in the fragrance of the salt-smelling moon and chopped onions frying in spluttering mustard oil, I asked Ma a question that had been bothering me for some time. I saw her shadow on the wall in front of us. The monsoon winds had arrived ripe in our little coastal city. Ma was combing my hair. Her voice punctuated the insistent sound of waves crashing against the shore.

She said to me, 'Mamoni, the world will tell you all sorts of things, but remember there's nothing wrong in choosing to be alone. Build a life for yourself, build a career, build a castle. Live in that castle alone, if you wish. The world will feed you dangerous ideas of romance and marriage and princes on white horses. Love yourself before you decide it's necessary to participate in the rat race of love.'

'Rat race, Ma? Black rats? White rats?'

'Rats come in all colours, my dear. Black, brown, white, beige. They are all rats. All equally important. Like people. We come in all colours, sizes and shapes too.'

'All shapes? Squares as well?'

'Squares, ovals, triangles, straight lines, pears, peaches, apples, hourglasses, circles. With two legs. With one-and-a-half legs—'

'Like you, Ma? With one full leg and another, um, almost full?'

'Indeed. We can have ten toes. Six toes. Eleven fingers. One eye. Two eyes. No eyes. It doesn't matt—'

'One eye? But aren't we supposed to have two?'

'We aren't *supposed* to have two, Mamoni. We can—but we might not. Even the Kolkata Biryani does not come with one prescribed recipe. You can make it any which way you like, if you remember to put the aloo in it. We are humans. We come in all forms too. As long as you have the aloo, you are okay.'

'Do I really come with a boiled, flavoured potato, like a handi of biryani? Why have I not seen it, Ma?

'The aloo is the soul of the Kolkata Biryani. You have yours too. Flavoured with sensitivity and understanding, curiosity and courage. Don't lose that light, that aloo, no matter what the stories tell you.'

'And can this aloo come in all forms? Creamy-mashed? Deep-fried? Parboiled?'

'Aloos can be whatever they want to be. And we need to respect them for who they are. Have you read the story of Cinderella's sister?'

'You mean Ella's ugly stepsister from the fairy tale?'

'What does it mean to be ugly, my dear? Was she brown like you and me? Were her eyes not blue enough to be compared to the heart of the ocean? Was her hair too kinky and black and wild?'

'My hair is black and wild, Ma! But you tell me I'm beautiful!'

'Because you are! Blue eyes, rosy cheeks, fair hair and size-zero figures are not the only standards of beauty, Mamoni. But maybe no one told Cinderella's sister that.'

# 2.

'Cinderella's sister lived with her mother, her stepfather, a younger sister and Cinderella in a little cottage on the fringes of a fair kingdom,' Ma told me. 'The cottage was big enough to house all of them, but not their soaring ambitions or sad histories. Memories of the past and incandescent dreams of the future were always at loggerheads in their household, cracking the walls of their cottage and their hearts into many fragments.'

'Incantotodreams, Ma?'

'Incandescent. I-N-C-A-N-D-E-S-C-E-N-T. Something that shines bright, Mamoni. With a burning intensity. Like the mother's burning need to save her two daughters. She wanted a life for them in which there were no tears or sadness, hunger or thirst. To her, a man with a fortune seemed to be the only solution to all her problems. And so, she began to raise her own daughters for high society, while she pushed away her stepdaughter, Cinderella, with a vengeance. She wanted no competition at all for her own children. Mummies and daddies are capable of making mistakes too.'

'You too, Ma?' I asked, as she tried to shift her weight from her left leg to the right.

'Yes, me too. And your Baba too. Just because we are older, we aren't necessarily wiser. And just because we were raised a certain way, we don't have to remain that way. Remember, all that is legal is not always ethical, Mamoni. And it is never too late to try and break free from cycles of hate. Unfortunately, Cinderella's stepmother could not.

'As a white woman who had married a poor brown man, much to the chagrin of her society, she had a hard life. The faraway continent she lived in was not ready for the union of a white lady and an immigrant, an indentured labourer from the land of snakes and snake charmers. They told her, "Love is not love if not between equals."

'So, when her husband died, she was left alone in a harsh world with two young girls to look after. She knew what it meant to be a single woman, unloved and unprotected. She wanted a better life for her daughters so they would not have to walk in and out of backdoors, trying to gain favours with the men in their town.

'When she met Cinderella's father, who was mourning the death of his wife, she found in him a kindred spirit. Yet, who knew that the grieving man, who loved his wife so dearly, would be ready to remarry before winter had melted into spring? But the man, indeed, was ready. He wanted someone to wipe his tears and warm his bed. And the poor woman with her little daughters was ready to call his hearth her home. After all, he was a white man with money and a dead wife. She had found in him an equal. Love, she assumed, would follow.

'The family moved into a little cottage on the fringes of the kingdom, built beside a gurgling, dimpled river. However, the step-mother could never bring herself to like her new husband's young daughter, Cinderella. She made Cinderella do all the household chores. It was her strange way of punishing the girl for the unfair treatment life had meted out to her when she was a lonely widow with two precious mouths to feed.

'The mother was very exacting with her own daughters as well. Her love and aspirations for them, especially for her firstborn, took strange dimensions. She wanted her eldest daughter to be ready to woo a charming man when the time came. So, Cinderella's sister had to go through gruelling hours of dance lessons every day until the calluses cracked under the soles of her feet. She learnt French, English and Bangla. She memorized verses from the holy books, and embroidered little handkerchiefs and silk pillowcases. In the winters, she knitted socks for her family; in the summers, she baked banana bread. She never played in the sun, and she couldn't go hiking with the boys. Her mother gave her special make-up tutorials to hide away any blemishes on her brown skin, and allowed her only two tiny meals a day to ensure that her fingers shrank enough to slip into any ring a rich man might offer her someday.

'So, Cinderella's sister grew up angry and bullied all her life, a brown girl among a sea of white faces with blue eyes. No matter how much she scrubbed, she couldn't get the melanin off her skin, or that beating voice of insecurity out of her heart. As her anger turned into bitter bile, she learned to bury herself under layers of skin-whitening cream and bleach and foundation and concealer and powder. And voila! Soon, the world forgot who she truly was. When they saw her pass by, they whispered: *"She has a fair face but her heart is dark as the night."'*

## 3.

'One day, the ruler of the land, where Cinderella's sister lived, decided to throw a fancy ball for his son, a fair young man born into gold and silver and raised to be an emperor. He drank from fountains of chocolate and slept on beds of soft feathers. The king invited all the beautiful young women of the land to the ball so his son could choose a bride from among the rows of lovely ladies in their flowing gowns and crippling corsets. The parents of these girls were ready to offer their daughters to the ruler and his son, like a sacrifice of tender lambs made to ancient gods.

'Cinderella's stepmother was well prepared to present her other daughter: a delicate girl whom she had carefully crafted like a prized project for a day so special.'

'Ma, is it true that this stepmother spilled a bowl of lentils in the ash before the ball and asked Ella to pick them out? And did the birds really help Ella?' I had read Ella's story before, and was eager to impress Ma!

'Well, it might just be true, my dear. The birds might have helped Cinderella because she was kind to them. She talked to them, she fed them, and she sang with them. They were her only friends when her father, her stepmother and her stepsisters refused to give her the time of day. Birds and animals are sentient beings. They return the love you give to them. You have heard of the faithfulness of dogs, the sensitivity of horses, and the empathy of elephants. Did you know that crows leave behind little gifts for people who feed them every day? Cinderella's birds might well have helped her pick out those lentils from the ashes! But the stepmother was relentless. The harder Cinderella worked, with or without her army of birds, the more demanding the stepmother got.

'A couple of days before the ball, Cinderella's sister picked out a rich cream-coloured gown for herself. It had long lace sleeves, a full tulle skirt, a velvet bodice, and a satin belt around the narrow waist. She was thrilled at the prospect of attending the festivities at the palace. She looked at her gown every now and then, afraid it would disappear if she didn't watch it closely. Unable to contain her excitement, Cinderella's sister slipped out of her coarse cotton dress the night before the ball, put on her gown and stepped out onto the starlit porch. The velvet sat soft on her body under the cold sky. Her eyes were like dark balls of fire, catching the silver of the moonlight. She smiled, hugged herself, and twirled barefoot on the wooden deck. Cinderella's sister imagined herself in the king's ballroom, dancing, dancing like burning flames among a sea of people. Her skin was flushed with joy. She felt truly happy and looked forward to the breaking dawn, perhaps for the first time in her life.'

'Did she like the young prince, Ma?'

'She had never met the prince, my love! So no, I don't think she liked the prince. But she loved the idea of dancing! She had read of enchanted gardens and gilded gates opening into endless corridors. She had heard of chandeliers that glittered like diamonds in the georgette sky. She had never seen anyone from another town or country before. She had never travelled to another kingdom. I think she simply wanted to go to the palace and meet people and have a good time. She was also probably hoping to eat some melt-in-the-mouth, soft, buttery Turkishdelight coated in sugar dust, or some exotic oysters. Oh yes, Cinderella's sister was excited to go to the king's palace.

'On the day of the ball, her mother forced her to eat three big bowls of deep-fried rice, two large buttered slices of rye bread, thick cubes of goat-milk cheese, a crackling shoulder of sheep, and a giant mutton cutlet. She wanted her daughter to feel very full. That way, she would only be able to nibble on a little marshmallow at the ball. What would the prince think of her if she ate a large piece of chocolate cake in front of him? Wanton girl! The mother shuddered—that would not do!

'Cinderella's sister felt positively sick by the time she forced herself into her corset and chemise and bolster and stockings and petticoat and heavy gown.

'"Keep your head lowered reverently at all times," her mother warned her, afraid of the fire in her daughter's eyes. "And no laughing out loud," she said, slapping the girl's cheeks repeatedly to add some colour to her face.

'After her stepmother and stepsisters left for the ball, Cinderella was alone in the kitchen with piles of dishes to wash, clothes to iron, and a dirty floor to scrub. She was covered in soot, as usual, wearing her frayed dress and a torn apron. Why can't Daddy help me? Cinderella wondered. The betrayal of her stepsisters and her stepmother hurt less than her daddy's silence. Cinderella cried and cried and cried, talking to the birds and singing to the dormice and doing the laundry.'

'Ma, is that when Ella decided to go to the tree she had planted by her mother's grave?'

'Yes, my dear. Some say the tree helped her. Others say a fairy godmother appeared. Either way, I think Cinderella had some help from her own mother, though she lay cold in the ground, long dead. Remember: the people we love never really leave us, even in death.

'Cinderella decided to put on her mother's taffeta gown, the only one she had been able to save from her stern stepmother. It smelled of old paper, and was a pale shade of Capri blue, gold and silver. She slipped into a pair of gorgeous slippers, the only gift from her father in many years, one that he must have forgotten about. Tying her long blonde hair into a bun, she pinched her pale cheeks for some colour, and rubbed a slice of beetroot to tint her lips red. The dress enhanced the cool blue shade of her eyes, and sat demurely on her white skin.'

'And then did the pumpkincarriage come to take her to the ball, Ma? The pumpkincarriage is my favourite part of the story!'

'It's more likely Cinderella got a lift from a kind stranger, my dear. And then, off she went to the king's palace! She did her best to stay away from her family, and channelled her energies toward the dance floor.'

'Did Ella like the prince, Ma?'

'She had never met the prince! So no, I don't think she liked the prince. But she loved the idea of dancing with him! She had always watched her stepsister dance and dance and dance in their backyard until her feet bled and her face glistened with sweat. She had heard her sister read aloud, in old English and medieval French, stories of enchanted gardens and gilded gates opening into endless corridors. She had heard from the birds of chandeliers that glittered like diamonds in the georgette sky. She had never seen anyone from another town or country before. She had never travelled to another kingdom. I think she simply wanted to go to the palace and meet people and have a good time, away from the soot and the cinder and the loneliness of the kitchen. She was also probably hoping to eat some melt-in-the-mouth, soft, buttery Turkishdelight coated in sugar dust, or some exotic oysters. Oh yes, Cinderella, like her sister, was excited to be at the king's court!'

# 4.

'Did the girls get to eat Turkishdelight, Ma?' I asked eagerly.

'The night turned out very differently for the two young women, Mamoni,' Ma replied. 'Cinderella's sister was constantly aware of her mother's sharp, watchful gaze, and the nagging pain in her belly from too much meat. She walked among the people, taking little hesitant steps, smiling timidly, afraid to falter, afraid to let her family down, afraid to be herself. She understood, for the first time in her life, the overwhelming tyranny of her mother's love.'

'The what, Ma?'

'The madness of her mother's love, Mamoni. Cinderella's sister spent most of the evening in a corner, watching the prince dance several dances with a girl dressed in a pale Capri blue, gold and silver dress. The girl in the prince's arms laughed too loud, cracked funny jokes, and seemed to be having the time of her life. Cinderella's sister, on the other hand, was yearning to break free. The corset was too tight, her mother too strict, the shoes she wore a size too small, the gown a little too large. She wanted to be back on the wooden porch of their little cottage by the dimpled brook, barefoot on a moonlit night. The king's ballroom was a far cry from the happy visions she had dreamt of the day before. She looked at the girl in the prince's arms and sighed.'

'Ma, was that girl Ella?'

'She was. And Cinderella felt truly happy and free that evening, Mamoni. There was nothing at stake for her. There was nothing to lose. There was no one holding her back. She danced with the prince, and she danced with the other noblemen. She found herself back in the arms of the prince several times during the night, gliding around the room. There was little time for conversation, the music was loud, the chatter and the clinking sounds of glasses and cutlery drowned their voices. The prince was transfixed by her slender, swanlike neck, it seemed. He hardly looked at her face. When his eyes strayed lower, Cinderella's fair skin reddened. She was embarrassed at how ill-bred the king's dear son was. He didn't care to ask for her name, and she didn't particularly want to divulge any information either. Cinderella was one with the birds that night, flying, soaring, dizzy with delight. All she cared about was the next dance. And the next. And the next ...

'Until the clock struck twelve, and Cinderella knew she had outlived her luck, she had tempted fate. How would she ever return to her little cottage by the bubbling river? If she could reclaim the night, she would. If she could reclaim those stPritis, she would. But young girls on dark roads are an invitation to goblin-men and pishachas that lurk in charnel houses. These beasts and formless men feed on the flesh of young women, creeping up on them stealthily from behind. Cinderella's mother, and her mother's mother, and her mother's mother's mother had warned her against the dangers of being a girl walking down the road alone at night. No other sight, they had said, was quite as terrifying and challenging and tempting to the world. There was not a single road at night for a girl to walk on, safe and free.

'Cinderella ran out of the palace, the skirt of her gown lifted up to her knee. What if the prince caught sight of her unstockinged calves? Cinderella did not care, she had to flee. A delicate shoe slipped off one of her feet, but Cinderella had no time to stop. Taking off the other slipper, she flew towards home. No matter how ruthless her stepmother was, at home, Cinderella was at least safe from the cruel desires of the creatures of the dark.

# 5.

'The next morning was somewhat strange for the women in that little cottage on the fringes of the kingdom,' Ma said. 'Cinderella's sister sat nursing blisters on her feet while her mother frowned and fretted. "Who was the girl the prince kept dancing with last night? Do you think you left a mark on him at all? What did he say to you when you danced that one time with him? Oh, why aren't things going according to plan? What are we to do now?"

'*Give me some space, mother. You're stifling me. Go away, please. Shut up...*

'There was so much Cinderella's sister wanted to say to the older woman, but she couldn't. Swallowing her words, stifling her tears, she let her mother fuss about the king's ball.

'Cinderella remained in the kitchen until late in the afternoon, alternating between bursts of wild energy and hours of daydreaming. At any rate, she made sure to stay away from her stepmother and stepsisters.

'Meanwhile, in the palace, the prince thought about the girl with the swanlike neck and the dainty feet. The next day, he sent out word through his father to the entire kingdom: "No one else shall my bride be, except the girl who from my arms ran free."

'The king's men went to every house in the kingdom carrying the pretty shoe that Cinderella had accidentally left behind. By the time they reached the cottage next to the stream, they had given up hope. Calling the man of the house out to the door, they explained the rule: "The prince will marry the woman whose foot fits in this shoe. We have searched high and low. We have been to the farthest corners of this kingdom. Speak! Do you have any young maidens in this little house of yours?"

'Cinderella's stepmother overheard the king's men and went to her beloved daughter, pinning her hopes on that single shoe.

'"But it wasn't my shoe, Mother," the young girl protested. She was terrified of her mother's machinations!

'Yet, a little voice in her heart whispered, *what if this shoe is your key to open the door that has locked you in? What if this shoe sets you free?* She closed her eyes, confused, bracing herself for what was to come. Her mother picked up a meat cleaver, shaved some skin off her daughter's ankle and cut off her big toe.

'Writhing in pain, Cinderella's sister hopped out of the door, feet wrapped in layers of stockings. She slipped into the shoe and the men rejoiced! Word was sent to the prince, who came on a white horse to take home his hesitant bride.

'Cinderella's sister, riding with the prince, thought to herself, *what kind of a man is he? Does he not remember the face of the woman he danced with? Did he not care to ask for her name? Why must I be betrothed to this man who is so callous and cold? How could I let my mother do this to me? All I wanted was to have a good time at the king's ball!*

'As the prince and Cinderella's sister entered a labyrinthine forest, the birds sang from the trees:

> *Tick tock two, tick tock two!*
> *There is blood in the li'l shoe.*
> *The shoe is too tight,*
> *This bride is not right!*

'Soon, the king's men came rushing to the prince, riding on their horses, gasping for breath. They had overheard a heated exchange between the old man and his wife who lived in the cottage by the stream. Having discovered the subterfuge, they told the prince that he had picked the wrong bride. Nobody but the prince was surprised by the revelation. He went back to the cottage, Cinderella's sister in tow. The young woman fainted in the doorway. She had lost too much blood, an infection gradually spreading through her left foot wrapped in layers of stockings.

'The shoe was offered to Cinderella next. It fit her perfectly and she rode off into the horizon with the prince after much ado. And the rest, as they say, is history.'

## 6.

My mother was looking out of the window, staring at the waves breaking on the shore. Where was the promise of happily ever afters in her version of the story? She was quiet for so long, lost in deep thought, that I had to nudge her and ask, 'Why do you sound so upset when you say that, Ma?'

'Because, my darling, Cinderella, like her stepsister, only wanted to have a good time at the king's ball! The prince was not part of their bargain. And for the first time, Cinderella's sister understood what Cinderella might have truly wanted in life; because she too had prayed for the same thing night after night: freedom.

'Yet, their moment of light and brief solidarity was followed by quick separation. There were no letters exchanged. No words. But something had changed in Cinderella's sister. She did not want to be a woman pulling other women down.'

'But Ma, how will the story work then? There's always an evil stepsister. Or a wicked witch.'

'Who is writing these stories, Mamoni? Can we not rewrite them? Why did Cinderella and her sister have to be pitted against each other for the hand of an indifferent prince? Could they not have been each other's support system? One another's strength? Could they not have been friends? They wanted to live in a different world, they hoped for a better future—good education, and money, and rooms of their own. They wanted to be able to walk down deserted roads at night without fearing for their lives.'

'And they wanted no prince, Ma?'

'No prince at all! They simply wanted to be able to eat Turkishdelight, unsupervised.'

'But how do you know all this, Ma?'

Ma looked at her left foot, partially amputated. I don't think I quite understood what her silence meant. My eyes went to Ma's legs. She always had a little trouble walking, but she still went with me to the icecream parlour whenever I wanted some black currant lollies. After a while I asked Ma, 'Can we rewrite Cinderella's story?'

'We can. We must, Mamoni.'

'Let's start at the very beginning then. What was Cinderella's sister's name, Ma?'

'Most women in history, my love, are anonymous. Let's give her a name. What would you like to call her?'

# Beat-Matching Beethoven

## *by Parita*

LOUD MUSIC. LOUDER BEATS. GYRATING BODIES. STROBE lights. Sweaty air.

It's like an earthquake!

'Oh my! It's the nightclub again! Dee, I tell ya …'

'Shabdo, I can shout at the top of my voice—people are shouting at the top of their voices! We all hear the same. Such a great leveller this place is …'

We are at Lat48°— also stylized as L'Attitude. Or just 'The Lat' to the partygoers—a cheap club with great music that actually has DJs who don't, erm, excuse my language, suck.

Most young adults would agree that the dance floor of a discotheque is where all the fun is at. For hard-of-hearing individuals like Dee, it is also a space which gives them the opportunity to be themselves. To talk aloud without having to worry about how loud you actually are. A chance to keep repeating 'What!' and not being stared down like a zombie.

But as for me and Lat48°? I call it The Latrine: always overcrowded, the place was originally a military hospital during the Second World War. Morbid. I hate it here.

'Dee, this is the last time this week. I get migraines at such places!'

'I lurrrve it ... this is liberating. Remember Towering Green and the shackles I was bound with? Look at me now! Woooh!'

'Pfff! I am going home!'

'You ain't going nowhere, mister.'

'I will turn deaf with all this loud noise!'

'Hahaha ... you are funny, Shabdo. You don't *turn* deaf, you *help* the deaf. Remember?'

Well, she is right about that.

~

I am Shabdo. I am a hearing aid. Full name: Sapta'k inc Shabdo 3D. But let's just go with Shabdo.

Dhwanii or Dee/D[1]—as I like to call her—is my companion, my partner-in-crime over the last few years. I am her prized possession and, well, I am possessive about her too. She owns me. Like o-w-n-s me.

I am supposed to be one of the smartest hearing aids available in the world. My job is to amplify voices: not those inside your head, but the actual ones. I am not the one to blow my own trumpet, but when people say, 'Shabdo made me hear again,' I do have moments of chest-thumping self-aggrandizement.

---

1  As a form of self-identification within the Deaf community, a capital D is used to identify someone who is culturally Deaf, while a lower case /d refers to someone who experiences a medical condition of hearing loss or is late deafened.

It is only incidental that Dhwanii's nickname happens to be D/Dee and it was always so. We will refer to her using a capital D, and this has no connection whatsoever to her being a 'd/Deaf' person.

Hearing aids like me witness several stories of joy and end-of-sorrows as people start to listen to sounds again—the voices of people they want to hear and even of those they want to avoid.

Dee was fifteen years old when I first heard her in Towering Green, a tall gloomy building in the suburbs, where Dhwanii was 'trapped' throughout her childhood.

Her laughter. That's the first thing I remember about Dee. She laughed like she didn't care. Utterly nonchalant with abundantly sprinkled notes of hysteria. She was shorter than early teens her age and had dark long hair. Her leg was in a cast. She was unkempt and unsure, but it was her explosive laughter that really intrigued me. I knew there were stories hidden somewhere in there. Of course, it took a while for me—'the creepy tiny hearing thing'—to get in her good books. It's been seven years since we escaped Towering Green, and I am still trying to unravel her.

Some days Dee is filled with glee, humming her favourite tunes, tapping her feet, clicking away on her keyboard, writing stories with abundant joy. But on others, she releases paroxysms of grief and breathes like a wounded animal. Sometimes, I just let her dwell and find the confidence to live and love in this normal and not-so-normal world that we tried to piece together. She may seem at peace at times, but most of the time, it is a fight.

Dee may seem a little over-enthusiastic at places such as this nightclub, but if you knew her story, you may understand why.

I, Shabdo, feel obliged to tell the story of this beautiful girl through my eyes. Or would it be ears?

∼

Once upon a time, when her fifth birthday was approaching, Dhwanii said to her father, 'Dad, I hope that I don't break any bones till next month. I really want to celebrate my birthday this year!'

Her father solemnly looked back at her with a meek smile—fourteen broken bones and three surgeries later, he didn't want to offer her false hope.

She was merely a kid when her mother passed, and his life had been tough too—crossing borders to find a 'good' job, then rushing back due to the demise of his wife, and then being left with a three-year-old with brittle bones to care for!

D's father had a penchant for classical music. He had an extensive collection of symphonies from the essential masters to the compositions of Mahler, Debussy, Tchaikovsky, Rachmaninoff. The usual. But mostly he leaned towards older baroque sounds—Handel, Vivaldi, Purcell ...

His evenings were filled with melancholy. He'd put on the music, and then proceed to pour himself a drink. Among the elite company of the classical greats, on one corner of the rack, there were two LP records of Manhar Udhas. They were never played, and no one talked about them. But Dee knew somehow—they were her mother's favourites.

Dee had always liked the noises of life around her, and her love of music was the only thing that she'd inherited from her dad (no one knows where bad genes come from).

D's first exposure to music was a sweet tune from a toy jukebox. The light notes, the repeating melody throughout—Dee could identify this music even in her sleep. Only much later she would realize it was a Beethoven composition, *Fur Elise*.

On the insistence of her grandmother, Dee's father married again. Soon after, her stepmother asserted that D should stay in a centre where she could receive the special care she required. Dee's bones were fragile like glass and broke with the slightest provocation—once it was a sneeze. Casts and braces had become like second skin. The neighbourhood was rife with rumours; someone called it the

'Dead Wife's Curse', while others conjured stories about 'the gene' she carried.

And so, the brutal architecture of Towering Green loomed in her future.

'But what if I fall and the nurses cannot help me?' the five-year-old asked her father.

'My girl, you are brave and strong. There will be no time when people won't be there to help you, and sometimes, all you need is the end of your own hand for support.'

'And you will come visit me?'

'Of course, my child. What else will I look forward to?'

Unbeknownst to him, her father was plying her with happiness and hope for the future. A better life when the clouds would have passed. He promised her that she would be getting a chance at freedom, at making friends, at being outside on her own, and at being normal—once she grew up.

'Slowly, your bones will gain strength. Probably by the time you become an adult, you would not fracture your bones as often, and you would be able to almost do everything as anyone else.'

The day of moving away was a sad one for D. The overcast sky resonated with her mood. It felt like her heart was being ripped out, yet she did not cry while bidding adieu to her father, thinking it was but a short stint of her life. As soon as she became an adult with stronger bones, she would be able to live with her father again. Fragile bones but hopes made of steel.

She focused on the surrounding noises for comfort and companionship. The wind that swished when she rolled down the window of the car, the splash of the water in the puddles they passed, the honking of the vehicles around her—the sounds of life made her forget troubles of her own.

Divided by disabilities but bound by fate, the centre was where 'challenged' kids grew up. It was a place far far away from the city, overlooking marshland between the creek and the salt fields. The three-storied Towering Green was a tall building to little D. It had few windows and scarce natural light. Long corridors and passages ensured that the place looked as sinister as it was; if you were wearing me, maybe the footsteps would echo.

In sync with the architecture, the head nurse at Towering Green was oppressive and ruthless. She was hardly bothered about the way the children lived. So long as she received the money to run the place, she continued ticking the health reports of the kids in her care. Her towering personality and thundering footsteps down the hallways made children run away. Dee tried her best to stay away from her.

As time went on, her father's visits became less frequent, but she looked forward to them. When he did come, he came bearing gifts—among them, always new music and sounds for Dee to listen to.

~

'*Rapunzzlll ... Raa-aaa-pppuu-nzzzllllll.*'

Dee was trying to get some sleep after our night out, but voices from nowhere are calling out to her—*Raa-punnnzeelllll ...*

'Oh Dee, sorry, my amplifier has gone crazy and is making that shrill sound.'

'Shut up, Shabdo!'

'Please take me off, milady. You have been asleep for a while now ...'

'Yes, but you behave too. Don't scare me with that piercing whistle! I get nightmares whenever I hear that sound.'

'You know what you gotta do, love. Reduce on that clubbing and send me off for servicing for a few days.'

'I'll think about it. Now, let me sleep.'

'What nightmares, by the way?'

'Oh the same—the children mocking me at Towering Green. The same haunting visions of long dark corridors, narrow stairs.'

Dee and I, we share an almost symbiotic relationship—she provides me with her deepest fears, and I provide her a brighter version of the sounds of life.

'Shabdo …'

'I am listening D.'

We were lying down on the bed staring at the roof. It was another ancient night of blue starry skies and Van Goghian palettes.

'Do you remember when I was trying to read the lips of the kids at Towering Green? That was when I learnt all the bad words!'

'Oh yeah, Dee. Fun times those were.'

'I especially remember how you kept nudging me to hear the subtle consonants …'

'I surprised you when I could make you hear the nuances of the silent letters.'

'Yes, surprised and elated!'

'I knew we were a match made in heaven!'

She smiled: 'That is true, dear Shabdo. If I knew that I'd have to live with you all my life, I wonder if I would have made your life so difficult at the start.'

'Teething troubles. False starts. Happens … And oh! You called me a "creepy tiny whistling ear-piercing thing", remember?'

'Oh yes, that you were and are. I used to feel so stuffy when I started wearing you. My ears used to choke! And then the shrill whistle that you make …'

'It was only when I started giving you some understanding of sound and noise that you decided you could be my friend.'

'Oh, Shabdo, I never had a friend during childhood. You know how kids reacted when a bedridden girl asked to play with them. You probably were my first friend. Well, maybe second, after *Fur Elise*.'

'Fur ... c'mon, a song can't be a friend for a deaf person.'

'Haha, but then neither can I be talking to a hearing aid!'

~

'Rapunzel, Rapunzel, let down your hair,' mocked the children around her.

With no special attention to hygiene or development, D did not receive haircuts and lived like a destitute child. She yearned to make friends but was not interested in the activities around her or the children who laughed at her long hair and tiny frame.

She kept thinking about Rapunzel's story and how a prince came to her rescue and they ran away to their 'happily ever after'. Away from the evil tower, life was filled with endless possibilities. Fairy-tale princesses have their knights in shining armour but has a true love's kiss ever solved congenital calamities? What do people in real life have? Would she ever get the chance to run away from this place?

The only person who was kind to her at Towering Green was a young caretaker called Josephine. A dark-skinned frail figure, overworked and tired, her eyes always radiated kindness. During naptime in the hot afternoons, Josephine would be busy with tasks, but for a few minutes she would sit down on the floor, leaning against the wall. The other kids would sleep, but Dee just lay there, her eyes wide open. Josephine would look at her and sing in a low voice. She was afraid of being heard, so she sang just loud enough for both of them to hear. Afterwards, Josephine would wipe away a tear and get up silently to continue with her work.

Till the age of twelve, casts from broken bones bound up most of Dee's time and did not allow her any freedom, even within the tower. On rare afternoons, hot winds would rise from the salt pans and the air would smell of salt. The noise of the creaking windows, the tolling of the faraway church bell, a lawn mower, the hurried footsteps of the Head Nurse, the thumps of children falling over—all these sounds presented to Dee the picture of normal life around her.

Another source of solace was a gift from her father: a Sony Discman[2] and a collection of CDs of classical lullabies—Brahms, Bach, Mozart, Beethoven, Chopin. And Erik Satie. This kept Dee quite busy. *When I hear music, I fear no danger*, Dee would think. *Life seems rosy and full of promises of the future. Music is my window to the outside world.*

Meanwhile, life kept passing by. With sincere hope, Dee kept awaiting her chance at happiness. Her time in the whole scheme of things. 'Nothing can go wrong from here!' was her optimism speaking. 'It is just a matter of time, I need to be patient. Happiness, Friends, Life … awaits me.' She had all her hopes and joy pinned to the future.

One June day, Dee said to her father during one of his visits: 'I don't like the monsoons, Dad!'

'Why, Dhwanii? The grass is so green and don't you love the pitter-patter of the rains?'

'But, Dad, there's also torrential thunder and the zap of the lightning. I get so scared at night.'

'Turn this into something meaningful, my dear.'

'What do you mean?'

'Like if you were at home, wouldn't you have tried to reproduce the sound of the rain using a bag full of spoons?'

'Oh yes, Dad. I can imagine that! Some spoons, a huge plate, and of course I would also use the brass pots that our kitchen is filled with.'

'Err. Those pots are not there anymore. But sure, why not?'

---

2  Discman was Sony's brand name for portable CD players. In 1997 the name was changed to 'CD Walkman' worldwide to match the cassette Walkman branding.

'Ha, wonderful, Dad. I am just wondering how different I will find home when I come back!'

I probably don't need to put this in words, but Dee was a dreamer. She dreamt of playing on green grass under blue skies, forgetting that by the time she might be allowed out of the tower, she would likely have passed that age. 'Someday when I grow up, and my bones become strong, I will,' was her respite from all things denied.

But life, as I know, is a complex series of events. Much more complicated than the circuits within my body. By the time Dee reached the age of fifteen, her bones had started gaining strength, but her hearing started to fade away. Osteogenesis imperfecta is a chronic condition, meaning it stays with you, and shows itself in different forms throughout your life.

The sounds of life that she was so used to started disappearing. She tried imagining it was all a nightmare and that she would soon wake up to the ringing alarm clock.

Gradually, though, even music lost its charm. The notes did not sound the same. She turned up the volume of her Discman, tried pressing the headphones closer to her ears, but it did not sound the same. She experienced words being spoken around her but was not able to comprehend them. People started shouting at her unnecessarily, and she ended all conversations with a 'WHAT?' But the high-volume replies didn't help her. The lawn-mower's *TRRR* she could hear, but she couldn't hear the DING of the church bells anymore. She knew and was afraid that something was wrong.

It was a cold, windy December, and she was very close to completing a whole year of no fractures, when certain notes dropped from her hearing altogether. 'My ears are hurting more than usual; can you please help?' she pleaded with the Head Nurse. But there was no help at hand; her father had only been providing the finances for her survival there and his visits had been less frequent than annual in the last few years.

Her dreams had started turning into nightmares—where instead of green grass she saw the ground beneath her feet being snatched away. The constant buzzing and ear-ringing had left her with no choice but to keep music away, too.

With sounds making their slow exit, Dee too faded away into her quiet world. She had to give up the thing that she cared the most for. Was this the end of her happiness? She wondered how it might be to live with complete hearing loss. Would it be full of chaos or would the quiet world bring respite?

~

'Are you listening, Shabdo …'

'Listening, D …'

'Do you know what my name means?'

'Dhwanii …? It means sound … *dhwanii* ... sound or echo … *dhun*[3] … music … tune.'

'Isn't that the most ironic joke of all time?'

'Well, not really.'

*Fur Elise* was her comfort music and today, it was playing in the background. She turned to it when she needed to feel soothed.

'What do you like so much about this?' I asked.

'Oh, it's more than a tune. It is like a wave—it comes slowly towards me, rocks me with its playfulness, and then moves away, and yet again, in a loop, comes back with a lovely tranquillity. I see the tune, along with hearing it. Do you understand?'

'You mean, it is a sound that you can see?'

---

3. Dhun: Hindi:धुन; literally 'tune'

'Yes, I see its loudness, its comfort, its existence around me when I play it.' She was all words now. 'When Beethoven wrote this piece, he was actually going deaf. Maybe that is why I can relate more to this piece than others—I can see it, the way Beethoven probably did. Maybe being deaf gives one another perspective and vision of sound!'

~

Me and Dee, it wasn't friendship at first sight. The first time she saw me, she literally tried to break me with her fingers. Her father had gifted me to her after the Head Nurse kept complaining that Dee couldn't hear lunch calls or wake-up alarms! She even threatened to kick Dee out of Towering Green if her condition didn't improve.

But Dee being Dee did not take the change so easily. First, she could not believe the wonder of being able to hear again with the 'help' of something so small. Second, she did not want to accept that her life was taking a new turn. And somewhere inside, she was overwhelmed that she would have to rely on something to lead a normal life.

Should she pin her hopes on a tiny hearing aid?

'Which, I insist, you should use more often,' I said to her.

'I feel itchy. My ears feel stuffed. I can't keep you around all through the day!'

'But you will get used to me!'

'I don't want to get used to a whistling ear piercer!'

'Whoa, watch your mouth, little lady!'

'You watch yours, Shabdo!'

'What do you want? I am helping you, can't you see?'

'I can see very well. It is the hearing that is the problem.'

'Yes, so let me help you with that!'

'Why should I rely on you? Aren't you gonna leave me, like everything else?'

'Well, not as of now, and not so soon. I will stay as long as I can ...'

'Till I am out of Towering Green?'

'Yes, and maybe even beyond ...'

'Promise?'

'Promise!'

Despite knowing that she needed me, Dee was not ready. Just not as yet.

But after spending three years with her at Towering Green, it was time for me to make good on my promise. As Dee's eighteenth birthday approached, she had many thoughts of running away, and now the monetary gift from her father ensured she could finally do it.

She used the money to bribe the staff at Towering Green and made arrangements to catch the bus that passed through the suburb at 5 a.m., ensuring that no one could hear her, us, running away.

Away from the tower, Dee and I developed a new life together.[4] I believe certain relationships refine life truths. Especially the ones you tell yourself. One must listen to what the heart says. No technology will be able to assist you with that.

You see, being deaf takes some time getting used to. Unless you are born deaf. In fact, life may even seem fairer for those born deaf; for starters, *how can you miss something you never had*? Then, comes the other category—the ones born with a perfect sense of hearing into a world of sound, the late-deafened adults or hard-of-hearing individuals, like D.

---

4 I have stayed around Dee, hearing her and her world since she was fifteen. She has struggled with the transition from the world of sounds to total silence. But she gradually made peace with the growing quietness around her and also with me.

Losing a sense after having lived with it is cruel. Who would like to let go? To miss hearing all the sounds we hear: the sounds of nature, the hum of the refrigerator, the clickety-clack sounds of the keyboard, the chime of the phone when someone messages you, the honking vehicles, the buzzing traffic, the gentle breeze, the sound of laughter, friends calling out your name inviting you to play, voices of people, even random people, or your favourite actors speaking those favourite lines...

Speaking of favourite actors and favourite lines, for Dee that would be Erza Miller playing Patrick. How many times has she rewatched *The Perks of Being a Wallflower* on nights when she couldn't pin herself down? How many times has she wished Patrick would make his grand entry into the room and say, *'Hey, everyone! Everybody! Everyone, raise your glasses to Dhwanii.'*

~

It has been seven years since we ran away and settled down in the city, far away from Towering Green. When Dee first got her own place to stay, she made sure she had a room set up exclusively for music. Over the years she had collected much like her father. While digital music was convenient, she loved the analogue warmth. She also inherited her father's music collection—all of it. They were going to throw it out anyway. On one wall of the music room, she hung prints and photographs and album cover art. She got a portable reel-to-reel player, an audio cassette player, Nakamichi amplifiers, and a Dieter Rams' designed vintage Braun Audio 310 turntable-radio receiver combo. All from eBay.

She also got the best vintage speakers, and carefully selected all the cables and connections. She connected the visualizer to a big wall display so she could see the spectrum: the graphic representation of the music that was playing. The woofers and the wall speakers moved and vibrated to the rhythms even at very low volumes. Her visualization of music provided her with the ability to 'hear' the actual nuances of the tracks, the microtunes, the subtle pitches … no wonder she could see and feel the music rather than hear it. She soundproofed the room with meticulous care. This was audiophile-level stuff. A high-fidelity listening room. Overkill for a person suffering from hearing loss, if you ask me.

But that room was her haven. She was really herself in there. I still remember the day we put on the first test song after it was all set up—still remember the song even: Asha Puthli singing 'The Devil Is Loose!' How the lossless format sounds filled up the room. Glorious. I loved the music room as much as her. Loved being there more than any place in this world.

Over the years, Dee and I have tried living a normal life. We both took our time to adjust to the city noises, the traffic, the dense living, the support-less life.

Dee used to be an ill-kempt clumsy teenager with long hair. Now, she has just turned twenty-five and transformed into a charming, beautiful, confident young thing. Her boisterous laughter has been replaced by a pleasant toothy smile. Studying in a night school, working in a publishing house as a copyeditor during the day, she's turned into a responsible adult. My hearing-aid heart swells with a sense of pride as I see the way she has adjusted to life now.

The other day, we were at the Medical Superintendent's office— we had just got her disability certificate signed, and were waiting to get it stamped.

'D …?'

She looked gloomy. 'Shabdo … a little louder please …'

'What's wrong …?'

'Shabdo, even with your help it seems like I can't really hear at all now. All the noises are gone. This morning I was gargling. And there was no sound. I cannot hear my own humming.'

'But it has always been tough, right?'

'It was tough and we adjusted, Shabdo. And with time, we became smarter with adjustments. That helped, the small things. Like finding the correct seats in a room, facing the speaker, writing it down rather than talking, and of course, using the right technology like you. But now ...'

'Ah. Is it that bad?'

'I'm afraid it is, Shabdo! Till last week I could manage a phone call with your help even though it was difficult.'

'Oh ...'

'Shabdo, you know I thought my life would peak once my bones gained strength, but now, it seems like I've plateaued!'

'Plateaus are not some place we stay forever. We always strive and we always go beyond. That's what we've done so far. And exactly what we will do now too.'

'Well, I hope this journey continues being the crest that it seems it is. Sometimes, I worry that I will also stop hearing the thoughts in my mind. The tunes that I remember. The rhythms that I can reproduce.'

'Dee, you know you are a special child.'

'I am just another girl, Shabdo. Less than ordinary. Special is someone like Beethoven, who had a natural ability to craft masterpieces ...'

'You continued your life without missing a beat! You beat-matched Beethoven, I would say! That is special!'

She laughed. 'You charmer! Where would I be without your smooth talk?'

'I can be your prince charming, D.'

'Shut up, Shabdo!'

'Rapunzel, Rapunzel, let down your hair.' We finally realized what the fairy tale meant.

*Just let down your hair, just be yourself.*

Dee learnt it slow—but Dee did it all! She got away from Towering Green. She forgave her father for abandoning her and cared for him before his death. She literally let go of her hair—trimmed it short, and didn't give two hoots what the world thought when they saw me on her ears. She also let down her hair and went on her first date.

And now, we're back at Lat48° again.

The gyrating humans, the loud loud loud music. The DJ spinning. It is a 70s night and extra crowded. Extra noisy. Free flowing cocktails, and we're rocking it. Back from the service centre, the music now sounded good to me. And loud.

And Dee at the centre of it all with her new nose piercing.

And her new friend—she too with an identical piercing. They looked so good together. Them smiling together. Them using sign language to communicate.

They do not really need me here. It is too loud for me to be of use anyway. For the first time, I am really enjoying being here at Lat48°. And when Bob Seger's *Old Time Rock & Roll* comes blasting on, it sets the floor on fire—we've never felt more human. Yeah. me too—the silly tiny hearing thing.

So human. So *alive*.

# The Ugly Duckling

## by Rakshita Shekhar

THE JUNE RAINS HAD BEEN PLAYING THROUGHOUT the night. While they rested now, so did the ducklings: under the warm sun, on the soft, grassy canopy made by the rains, just for them. Next to them lay their mother, eyes wide open. She was trying to concentrate on the sound of the marsh water flowing, but all she could hear was the thumping of her heart. She spun, she swirled, she turned, and she twirled, until she could no longer try to rest. So she got up and decided to take a stroll, out to the well, near the farmer's house. She just wanted to swim, without a worry about her grey duckling. Grey—whose birth had shattered all her dreams.

Her life wasn't supposed to be like this, she often told herself. She had planned to be a good mother. Now she was tired of trying so hard to be one. She was sick of being worried, frustrated and melancholic all the time, and couldn't remember what she had been excited about when she was incubating her eggs.

As she swam in the cool marsh waters, she passed the little overgrowth, the one beside the big rock. It seemed like many eons ago when she had stood here, preening her feathers. She paused, looking back at the bush. She could still breathe in the memories of the November air—the November air that had brushed her neck as she had pumped her head up and down. The November air that had carried to her the scent of her drake, standing a few feet away.

He had responded by looking at her and then swiftly turning his head to show her his back. It was newly moulted. Just for her. She had screamed in decrescendos, one syllable, then two, flowing into several. He had grunted, and burped, and she had followed. It was as if he was, right this moment, craning his head up, raising his tail, and lifting his down up. She felt the excitement rushing back through her neck and jerked it from side to side rapidly, just like she had done that November day. She imagined flying to her drake, placing herself right in front of him and him preening the back of her wings as she continued singing the song of joy in her long-syllabled decrescendos.

A sudden wave from underneath jolted her out of her reverie. She continued swimming, but couldn't stop her mind from vividly seeing what had happened next. As she waded through towards clearer waters, tears rolled down her cheeks for the first time since her eggs had hatched.

In April, as the summer sun had entered the marsh, she had laid her eggs right where her babies now slept. Every day, she would sing her grunty songs, happy that her dream was coming true. She would hug the lotus and kiss the grass. She would sway with the sun and do the chasse. She planned the games she would play and the lessons she would teach.

One month later, a few hours after sunrise, five eggs hatched, all in quick succession. Together with their mother, all five ducklings happily quacked and flapped until they were tired. Then she had licked them good day and sent them off to the pond with their father, so they could bathe and eat.

If pain was inevitable, she wished now that she could trade her present pain for the one she had felt that day: missing the opportunity to have memories of her ducklings' first swim. It had been a seething pain, but it had been healed by her determination to run the last mile: the hatching of her last egg, the brown egg. But now, she couldn't see the finish line at all.

The warm tears on her cheeks cooled the contours of her beak, and allowed them to droop.

Her brown egg had hatched three full days after the first five. Out from the brown egg had come a beautiful grey baby, unlike the brown with bright orange legs and feet that she had always seen. The jet-black beak added to the ethereal vulnerability she knew instantly would be hard to protect.

For the first twenty-four hours, Grey was very clumsy and couldn't leave the nest to eat. But when he did begin eating the next day, everyone burst into laughter. It was as if they were witnessing a cute monster eating. Upon finding young shoots of *neel kamal*, he would bury his long neck inside the water and stir vigorously, causing the shoots of plants, as well as some invertebrates to begin floating. Then he would pick up only the *neel kamal* shoots with his beak and, with the help of his rather large feet, tear them apart, before chewing. Unlike the rest of the flock, he wouldn't forage under rocks for larvae and preferred uprooting plants to catching small fish, crabs and snails. When he stood, he cutely tucked his feet up on his back, watching over everything as if he were a guard. He was a quiet soul and loved to ride on his mother's back most of the day.

But as days grew into weeks, the word 'cute' had started fading from the mother duck's thoughts. Grey was growing much larger than his siblings. He could eat more than the entire flock. He still plucked shoots off their roots vigorously, wouldn't eat the floating vegetation or swimming invertebrates like the rest and couldn't break vegetation gently with his beak. His grunt sounded like an elephant blowing water from its trunk. When other animals came near the nest or the flock, he turned savagely aggressive. But most of all, he was very adamant, unwilling to adapt and learn.

Just two days ago, Grey had returned home with bloody feathers—for the fourth or fifth time. A troop of screaming ducklings had followed him. Two of the ducklings, one his sibling, were crying inconsolably. Upon arrival, Grey had silently walked up to a far corner and begun preening himself as if this troop—his mother, three of his siblings standing next to her with heads hanging in shame and another one protesting with the troop—were all events in an alternate universe that didn't concern him. While the mother duck had pondered over what emotion to pick for herself, she heard the words 'fight', 'squirrel', 'Grey attacked' and 'killed'. It hadn't taken her long to choose to agree with the majority. There was a perverse safety in numbers. So she had screamed her lungs out at Grey, who continued to lick his feathers, in his characteristic calm arrogance.

The mother duck sighed deeply and dove her head into the water. She couldn't understand Grey's odd behaviour. Her other ducklings were in a perpetual state of shame or anger or frustration. She herself had really become numb. Her anger was an act. Her frustration was a show. Her positive energy was a mask.

She rapidly moved her head from side to side, to make the water splash across her eyes, but along with it, her displaced feathers began rubbing irritatingly on her neck. She tried focusing on the eel passing under her but soon found she was wondering if the eel's mother worried about the eel too.

Some nosy flock elders had come around later to advise her. It would be better to expel Grey from the flock, they believed. They had said this many times before, but never in front of her ducklings.

'He behaves like he doesn't need the flock,' they had said in a caring and polite tone. Her little protestor had walked out with a 'you are a failure of a mother' expression on his face. Her traumatized duckling had clung to her, with a superstitious faith in her strength to handle this situation. The others had stood motionless, eyes glued onto their mother, as if waiting for her not to disappoint them again. Grey had sat emotionless. Just like her.

She tumbled and sprayed some water over her feathers. It felt good.

Yesterday, she had tried asking Grey why he felt a need to kill a harmless squirrel. All he said was that he didn't kill it. She had also tried finding out from her other ducklings what had happened. They had answered with counter questions: 'What do we do now?' 'We will be expelled if we continue to keep this monster at home!' 'Do you love us as much as you love him?' 'He does everything wrong and yet you don't scold him!' 'Do you never think of us?'

She opened her eyes slightly and saw a thin ray of sunlight travelling with her. She tumbled again, this time with more vigour, as if the momentum would carry her all the way to normalcy, and again, and again. With each movement, she swam forward, and eventually came upon the farmer's house.

Her drake had agreed with the flock elders. Not her. If only Grey would speak out, she thought; if only she could teach him the right way to interact with others. If only Grey had the right emotions at the right time; if only she could teach him to be a good duck; if only he became more like a duck and less like the way he was born—less *grey*.

She stepped out and walked on the soil. Aah! She hated the dry sand getting between her feet. She quickened her pace, imagining the cold spirals of the nearby well's water caressing them. She had heard a lot about the well. Now she could enjoy it.

She climbed down the steps and lay down on her back, then swiftly turned over so her feet were up in the air. She waded on her back until she was touching the wall. Then she quacked and put her ear to the walls, so she could hear herself reverberate. The wind gushing through the well swished past her head, moving the feathers on her neck in a dance.

She was giggling and quacking, feet up in the air, when she noticed two huge white birds flying right above her. They looked so magnificent and god-like that she immediately straightened up so she could see them properly. Their feathers were completely white. Their beaks were sunny orange with black bases, with black beauty marks directly above. Their long necks gave them a slender look.

The mother duck's wonder carried her out of the well and onto the edge of the blue river where little specks of white pearls danced around the birds, as they sailed with their necks bent in an S shape, their bodies completing the calligraphic stroke. The only sound she could hear from their flock was that of water being slapped by their black feet as they landed—a stark contrast from her loud and gregarious brood. Yet, it seemed like all the birds in the flock behaved in tandem with each other.

She looked around. They were all in pairs—mostly elders, but also some young couples. One of the pairs was standing just like Grey, with one leg tucked inside the feathers. Before she could raise her head fully to laugh at the coincidence, she saw it: two mothers with their young ones on their backs, just like her and Grey. Curious, she inched closer. The young ones were coloured grey. She could see some others eating. Just like Grey.

She immediately turned to go. It could not be, it could not be, it could not be. Grey had hatched in her nest! She hated the ickiness of the sand more than ever now and wished she could kick it so hard, that all of it would fly away to disappearance, forever. And yet, her pace along the dry sand and that of the grief engulfing her were poles apart.

The other ducklings in the flock called Grey names and imitated the way he grunted. They loved chasing him, for when he, much bigger than any of them, would take off and land a little farther, he would slap the water with his feet too. They teased him to no end. Even if one excused their behaviour as juvenile banter, it pained her to overhear the elders discuss how Grey could not be a duck. They didn't care that his singular presence prevented predators from nearing the flock. None noticed that Grey never turned his savage aggression towards the flock—it was reserved only for those who threatened his family.

Her Grey never lied. If he said he hadn't killed the squirrel, it must be the truth. Perhaps the squirrel was trying to steal the flock's food! But to her flock, it was Grey who represented the threat, not the predators.

Mother duck rubbed her wet, tired eyes, wondering how she could feel relaxed and tired at the same time through the act of crying. Perhaps it was the memories of her attempts to conform to the flock that tired her.

'Drink water from the river, not this marsh.' 'Feed Grey rabbit meat.' 'Teach him to quack like us.' 'Tie him to the tree when he behaves aggressively.' 'Push him away when he climbs onto your back.' 'Your soft-heartedness is spoiling him further.' 'Think about your other ducklings. They're suffering because of Grey too.'

Ever since the day Grey had ventured out into the marsh, mother duck's dreams had been consumed by shrieks of crying, of visuals of too many ducks jumping on bouncy sand, of leaves fluttering around them angrily, of raindrops hitting them hard, raindrops that had lost their vertex. She craved quiet inside her head.

Her ducklings were waiting for her when she returned from the farm. The five crowded her and began pecking at her underbelly. Grey climbed onto her back and started preening her feathers. 'See, he cares!' she screamed to the flock elders inside her head. It felt good, a little guilt dusted off. She kissed and caressed all her babies, rolled in the mud with them, bathed them and fed them. As they all played together, Grey silently sitting on her back, she allowed herself to jump many years forward and for the first time, she liked what she saw. Her five, with their mates and young ones on the marsh, swimming gleefully under Grey's protection, now huge, white and magnificent, with his mate by his side. And their grey little young ones, swimming with the ducks …

All of a sudden, she wanted to go back to the blue river so she could imagine better.

And so she did. Every day, for a week, she visited the quiet breed of swans known as Mute Swans while her babies napped in the noon. She observed keenly, for she had to teach Grey.

Or perhaps, she thought one day, should she leave it to the swan flock to teach him?

She brought Grey along the next week.

On the first day, Grey refused to go near the river. So the mother duck took him to the well instead. The magic happened there, just like it had for her. Grey witnessed the birds flying above and became curious. Mother and Grey climbed out of the well and followed the birds to the riverbed. They stayed there for hardly five minutes before Grey wanted to go back to the marsh.

The next day was better. They watched the birds take off and land for a whole hour in silence. Even her mind had obeyed. And for the first time, she had been able to look at Grey and feel pride. He was naturally handsome, elegant, caring, loyal and resilient. She hadn't taught him to be any of these things. On their return journey, while she prepared to go back to her noisy flock, a thought struck her suddenly: had the flock's noisy environment infected Grey's naturally silent mind and made him like her—trapped in noise?

On the fifth day, Grey courageously ventured out to the swan flock. The mother was the one hiding this time, afraid she would be mistaken for an intruder. But her instincts told her that Grey would be fine. The swans were squatting on the big rock in the centre of the river. Some were flapping, some were clucking, some twiddling with twigs. Grey sailed with a calm determination no one had ever seen in him. Mother duck watched with bated breath as he approached the rock.

As Grey climbed up, there was a very brief break in the almost invisible pattern the flock was sitting in. Grey, very confidently, took up the spot where the break was made, completing the pattern once again. Mother was shocked. 'How did he know to do that? She herself had only noticed the break when Grey joined them! He was even bobbing his head and wiggling his tail in the same rhythm as the rest, as if he knew the steps to the dance! Or was it the way they communicated with or instructed Grey, she wondered.

When the flock got down from the rock to swim again, an elder swan silently guided Grey into position by blocking his way to the paths he was not allowed to take—instead of shouting and correcting him. The swans always maintained a pattern or rhythm, making it easier perhaps for Grey to understand the expectations. They also never came too close to him. This reminded her of the innumerable times that Grey had become jumpy and irritable while swimming with the duck flock. The ducks liked to be close, perhaps too close for comfort for him. But she had always tried to teach him to be more adjusting. Now, she knew it was just the swans' way of being. These swans had a different language, a different culture.

Grey instinctively understood that. In turn, the swans knew how to make him happy.

'Look how Grey is doing here, without anyone's reminders, and without any punishments,' she said to an invisible flock of ducks in front of her.

A voice inside her replied, 'Yes. It seems like he doesn't belong among the ducks. Perhaps he will be happier with the swans.'

Just then, Grey turned and called out to her. Hesitatingly, mother duck swam up to the swan flock. She didn't know how to gPriti them, or how to talk to them. Perhaps Grey had felt like this among the duck flock?

Mother duck bent her head in respect, hoping she wouldn't have to endure what poor Grey did among the spot-billed ducks. Grey hopped onto her back and said, 'Let's go home.' The swans quickly filled up the spot that he'd vacated.

Mother duck's heart filled with happiness and determination again as she thanked the swan flock in her own language, hoping they would understand, and turned to go. As she and her swan swam back, Grey grunted and hissed all the way. Far from sounding like an elephant to her, this time he sounded like a happy Grey, like a stress-free Grey. She could feel his feathers smoothened out over her. For many days she had wondered why they had been standing oddly. 'Perhaps out of unhappiness?' she thought now. Did that mean he was not emotionless and arrogant, her little Grey? Did that mean she just hadn't understood his communication?

Now, Grey had a new beat about him and mother duck had a new dream. She could clearly see her grand finish line: a stress-free and confident Grey. She needed to keep him safe, even mentally. For this, she needed to attend to all her ducklings. Make them feel safe and valued. So they would in turn appreciate why Grey needed to feel safe and valued. They all had to learn from the swan flock about

Grey's language and culture. They all had to stand tall in the face of others trying to shame them but also muster empathy for the duck flock and educate them. Most importantly, she had to let Grey learn from his second flock how to truly be himself.

She was indeed a good mother, for she was ready again, for many more mothering milestones, and resolute again, for the new future that lay ahead.

# The Deaf Snow White

## *by Kanika Agarwal*

THE GREAT KING AND HIS QUEEN WERE MARRIED FOR five years and were still waiting for a child. The mother often prayed for a girl whose skin and heart would be white and pure as snow. In their sixth year, their prayers were answered and they finally got a baby girl. However, the queen died a month after the birth of the child. The king was left to care for their only daughter and put his heart and soul into it. He named her Snow White in remembrance of his wife's wishes.

As the years passed by, Snow White blossomed into a beautiful girl fair as snow. She had a gentle heart and a soothing voice. She grew up playing in the gardens of their palace, and most of her friends were the plants, bushes and her favourite three little birds—Brownie, Bluie and Ruie. She talked to them endlessly as her father presided over his court. Days turned into months and months turned into years. In the blink of an eye, Snow White was ten years old. It was then that she started losing her hearing. Her father knew

97

that he would not be able to care for Snow White alone now. So, he remarried—primarily to provide care to his deaf daughter. But no one knew what fate had in store for Snow White.

Over time, Snow White realized that her new mother was not really her friend. Snow White received kindness from the queen only in her father's presence. Whenever her father was away the queen made Snow White her personal caretaker. She would make Snow White clean her special gowns, give her bodymassages and tend to her personal needs. The favourite pastime of Snow White's two stepsisters was to make fun of her. They would pull her frock or hair if they wanted to get her attention. Once, Snow White gave them a disdainful look. But one of the stepsisters made an innocent face and moved her lips slowly for Snow White to read, 'Sweet Sister, that is the only way to get your attention with your deafness, no?'

Many times, Snow White wanted to go to her father and tell him of her true plight. However, the queen would often move her lips to say, 'One word to your father about this and I will make sure that the palace knights abduct and devour you the next time your father goes away.' This scared Snow White to no end and she would keep a smiling face in front of her father all the time.

If Snow White ever happened to try and make new friends, her stepmother would cruelly remind her of her deafness and her inability to communicate.

'So, what if I can't hear? I can speak and express myself to people. My friends can listen to me,' Snow White once tried reasoning.

But the queen made a face. 'Who would want to listen to a disabled person!'

This tore Snow White's heart to pieces. Self-esteem and confidence were alien terms to Snow White as she grew up. All she knew was to dream and wish and talk to her birds, 'How I wish I could live a jovial kind of life like those girls in the neighbourhood.' The birds would sit on her shoulder and chirp in an attempt to comfort her.

Snow White was thankful that the birds at least understood her and gave her such serene communication.

Snow White started sensing that her stepmother was using her deafness to fill her father's ears against her. She observed that her father had become sterner towards her. He once came and sat beside her to talk. She saw his lips moving: 'My dear little child, you need to work harder and make sure you treat your mother and your sisters fairly.'

For a moment, Snow White almost burst into tears and blurted out the truth, 'Am I the cruel one, Father?' But she recalled her stepmother's threat and restrained herself, 'I am sorry, Father. I will be more careful in the future.'

~

Years passed, but nothing improved. One day, while her father was out on yet another long trip, the cook fell sick and the whole responsibility of the kitchen was handed over to Snow White. One morning, while Snow White was busy with some work in the backyard, a bucket of water fell with a thud in the kitchen. Snow White did not hear the noise and continued with her work. The queen got angry and lashed out at Snow White mercilessly. She yelled at her, 'You have become too lazy. Your deafness deserves this.' Snow White ran out of the house. She had no idea where she would go. But she was so scared that she kept running in whichever direction she could see.

After running for almost an hour, she came across a small but beautiful cabin in a forest. She stopped at the door huffing and puffing. Despite being breathless, the beauty of the house mesmerized her and her heart skipped a beat. The door of the house barely reached her waist. She wondered who could live in such a small house. At first, she was sceptical of approaching anyone. But her fatigue soon took over her fear. She rang the bell of the house, hoping someone would open the door. But there was no response. She rang the doorbell five times before she decided to check the doorknob. To her surprise, the door wasn't locked. She opened the door and crawled inside the tiny hole of a house.

The house looked neat and tidy. Everything was of shrunken size. It looked like the dollhouse that Snow White always saw her stepsister playing with. As she moved her gaze around, she saw a shelf with many books, a spic and span kitchen, and a dining table full of food. The meal was laid out on seven tiny plates. Snow White could not resist the temptation. She had been working the whole morning and had forgotten to eat. After having run away from her cruel step mother, she had forgotten all about her hunger. But now that she saw food, her stomach growled. She ate almost all the food and moved ahead to see what lay in the other rooms. As she moved, she found a room with seven beds. She was so big that she alone could occupy all the seven beds and still have no room to stretch. Exhausted, she curled up on the beds anyway and quickly drifted into a slumber.

So it was that seven little people came home and found their dinner plates empty. 'The maid must have let some of her friends in and finished our dinner,' snarled one of them. Yet another said, 'The maid has been cooking for us forever and this has never happened before. It must be some witch.'

Tabish, the eldest of them spoke, 'The bedroom door looks open. There might be someone in there. Let's check.' When they all entered the bedroom, they found Snow White sleeping.

'An intruder! Let's kill her!' shouted one of them.

Tabish stopped him. 'No! She looks harmless. Had she wanted to harm us, she would have been hiding somewhere, waiting for us.' They started making noises to wake her up, but to no avail. Tabish advised them to cook dinner while waiting for the girl to wake up. So everyone went about the house preparing dinner.

Snow White woke up to the pecks of her little birds on her body. 'How did you find me?' she asked. They rubbed their beaks against her nose sweetly. Suddenly, Snow White realized that someone was in the house. She peeped out of the bedroom door to find seven little people sipping wine by the fire. She was scared of what awaited her and wanted to run out. So, she tried tiptoeing, only to realize that she was too big to escape the house unnoticed.

She spoke up hesitantly, apologizing to them for her intrusion and tried walking away. They moved their lips but they were too tiny for her to read. That is when she had to tell them about her deafness. While many of them did not believe her and accused her of lying, one of them, Sheram, gestured to her to sit and explain her story. Tabish and Sheram listened patiently. By the time she finished her story, her fear had turned into grief and she sobbed inconsolably.

Tabish wrote on a piece of paper: *You can stay with us. But you will have to cook for us and take care of the house. We will go to the forest and fetch food and wood every day.* Snow White immediately and happily agreed. Sheram added to the note: *There are some hidden shelves in this house that you must not touch or try to open if you ever happen to find them.*

'I will not.'

*'And tell your birds not to shit inside the house.'*

Everyone laughed at this, including Snow White.

Given Snow White's dedication, it didn't take time for her to bond with the little people. They soon became a family. However, there were times when Snow White would talk to her birds, 'I wonder if my new family members speak about me behind my back too. It is so difficult to even read their lips. Do they talk in some secret language to keep me away?'

Meanwhile, the king came back from his trip and started worrying about his daughter. He announced, 'Anyone who brings my daughter back to me shall get a reward of a hundred gold coins.' The word reached the seven little people. They went to their house that evening and told Snow White about it.

She said, 'While I do miss my father, I do not wish to go back to my cruel stepmother.' They never asked her to leave again, but they made sure to keep updating her on every announcement that her father made.

The next afternoon, Snow White found herself talking to her birds, 'Why did they mention my father? Perhaps they want me to leave!'

Snow White's stepmother soon discovered through one of her secret guards that Snow White was hidden in the forest. Before the king could find out, she decided to end the trouble once and for all.

One day, when the seven little people were away, she went to the little house disguised as a disabled woman. She sat by the house and started sobbing loudly. Snow White heard nothing. So, the stepmother sat right opposite the window and sobbed loudly. As Snow White continued with her household chores, her gaze fell on the sobbing woman.

She went out and said, 'Why are you crying?' The disabled woman said something but Snow White found it difficult to read her wrinkled lips. Snow White presented her with a paper and pen and said, 'I can't hear. Do you mind writing to me?'

'You can't hear? Oh, dear!' She made a pitiful face and pointed at her leg, trying to say that one of her legs was missing. Snow White felt pity for the woman. The old woman then showed her a worn-out picture of a child. She then wrote: '*This is my son. He kicked me out of the house because I am disabled. I have learnt that this world is no place for people with disabilities. Come, let us both drink this poison and die. Heaven is our only abode.*'

Snow White's eyes widened. She moved away from the woman saying, 'I don't want to die. I am too young.'

The old woman carried on writing in her messy cursive: '*Look at me. I am disabled as well as old. Do you want to suffer like me in the future?*'

Snow White started thinking, *The woman is right. People with disabilities suffer a lot. I have seen how cruelly people have treated my deafness. I should drink the poison with her before I have to suffer the dual distress of old age and disability.* She finally replied, 'You are right, dear old woman. I have suffered in the past and may suffer in the future too. Death looks like the easiest way out. Come let's drink ourselves to death.'

'*That's my brave girl. I am happy that I will have some company after death. I have two bottles. You drink first.*'

Snow White gulped down the bottle in one go and fell dead on the floor. The stepmother ran away satisfied with her victory.

Soon afterwards, the little people came upon the dead body of Snow White, led by Brownie and Bluie. Tabish said, 'She has been poisoned. Look at her throat.' Everyone stared at her blue throat. Tabish knew the right potion for it. He went to the kitchen, brought down the potion from one of the hidden shelves and gave it to Snow White. She woke up startled.

Snow White looked around but found no trace of the crippled woman. She started thinking, *If I tell them about the disabled woman, they will laugh at me. How should I prove my words?*

'Who gave you the poison?' asked one of the little people.

'I drank it myself. People with disabilities get no respect in this world. Death is a better option.'

'And who said that to you?'

'Nobody. I have experienced it all in my life.'

'Don't talk nonsense and get our dinner ready. We are hungry.'

Snow White went to the kitchen quietly and started cooking, mumbling at her birds, enraged, 'Couldn't they even let me die? They talk about me behind my back, give me food like a beggar and want to send me away. Now that I am leaving, they again want to have control over my life!' She cried a lot that night. In her outpouring of emotions, she never gave a thought as to what may have become of the old woman or why she couldn't find her upon waking up.

~

The next day, on their way through the woods, the seven little people started talking about Snow White.

'I have observed that Snow White feels lonely at times.'

'We need to find a way to communicate better with her. Writing is too slow and limits us.'

'I once stumbled upon a deaf family. They were talking to each other with their hands instead of their mouths. It is known as sign language. We should teach that to Snow White too.'

'But Snow White can speak. What use will sign language be to her?'

Tabish said, 'That is indeed right. We should be the ones learning to sign for Snow White. However, if she doesn't know the signs, our learning will be futile. So, let us all learn sign language together.'

With that, they decided to meet the deaf family after work. As dusk crept in, they headed towards the deaf family's house.

As they reached the house door, they were surprised to see a lantern at the foot of the door. In the place of a knocking handle, there was a board that said: 'Deaf family. Do not knock. Flash the lantern at the window instead and the door will be answered. As they flashed the lantern, a cute child, who was about a foot tall, danced his way to the door.

After introductions and listening to the story of the seven little men, Salla the deaf father spoke and gestured, 'It would be good for all of you to learn sign language. However, only sign language will not suffice. You all need to understand Deaf Culture so that Snow White can live a better life.'

Tabish wrote: '*So, how do we start? Can you spare enough time for Snow White and us?*'

'Let's start tomorrow? My son can come to your house to start. He and Snow White are around the same age and might enjoy each other's company.'

The next day, Tabish introduced Snow White to Salla's deaf son, Shals. Snow White wondered what was happening. She was baffled to see someone move their hands and communicate without using their voice at all. Tabish sensed her confusion and handed over an explanatory note to Snow White—

*This kid is deaf, so are his parents. They live nearby. They do not speak. They communicate using sign language. We thought that learning a new language would make our evenings more refreshing and we could also make new friends. So, would you like to join us in learning something new?*

Snow White agreed and they all started learning sign language together. She also met Salla and his wife occasionally. But she preferred talking to Shals. Within no time the little men and Snow White became good at signing. Thereafter, Snow White started spending more time with Shals. She would finish her chores and visit his home or call him over to her house. They would chat endlessly about things ranging from the forests to Deafness. Snow White loved learning about the Deaf Community. She soon started taking lessons in Khuzdul—the language of the little men—with Shals so that she could read the books on Deafness that she so often saw on the shelves in their home.

One day, while reading one of the books, Snow White realized that there was diversity within the Deaf Community. 'You and I are the examples of that diversity,' explained Shals. 'I am genetically deaf, while you are a post-lingual deaf,' he said. 'There are many more kinds of people with Deafness.'

Suddenly, Snow White felt as if a great stone had been lifted off her chest. To know that there were many others like her seemed to make the world a much safer place now. At the same time, she thought of herself as foolish for not having thought about this heterogeneity when she'd met the Deaf family for the first time.

'So, how do they all communicate with people? Do all of them learn sign language?' asked Snow White.

'Not really! Some prefer to stay with oralism while others like to try and experiment with sign language and the "D" environment or Deaf Culture. It depends on a lot of factors like their degree of deafness, personal preference and societal impact.'

One day, while reading a book, her heart skipped a beat and she found herself dreaming of hearing everyone's speech like her old days. When Shals came to her house, she asked him about cochlear implants, 'Can it really help us hear? If I get it, will I get my hearing back?'

'Cochlear implants are highly subjective to individuals. While some people can benefit from it, many can't.'

Snow White's dreams came crashing down. Looking at her, Shals added, 'Hearing is not the only thing needed to thrive in this world. I have many signing friends across the world who have made their own mark in the world. I will give you a book on it tomorrow.'

The next day, as Snow White began reading her new book, she found more joy in signing. She decided to delve deeper into the signing community. Slowly, Snow White found herself so mesmerized by the deaf community and the visual richness of sign language, that she decided to become a committed signer.

~

Seeing the little people and Snow White signing, many others in the forests started signing, too. In no time, Snow White felt as if she was in heaven. This gave Snow White and Shals confidence to spread more awareness about sign language and they started approaching people, trying to convince them to learn sign language.

Soon word about sign language and the 'Deaf Duo' spread in the town too. The evil queen heard this and was startled. She thought to herself, *It cannot be Snow White. Snow White is dead.* But the uneasiness did not let go of her. She decided to send a guard and find out about the Deaf Duo. When the guard told her about Shals and the beautiful deaf girl with him, the queen became worried.

She devised another plan. She disguised herself as a man and her maid as a deaf woman. They both went to the forest and found the little men's cabin. They started quarrelling in front of the cabin. To grab Snow White's attention, they threw a few stones inside the house.

Snow White and Shals were chatting as usual when they saw the stones coming in through the window. They decided to go out and have a look. There, they found a couple quarrelling awkwardly. The queen hit the maid shouting, 'You are no good.' When Shals tried to stop the queen, she looked at Snow White and gestured, 'She is my wife. She is deaf. How can a hearing person like me deserve such a vile creature?'

'Mind your language. You can't call her vile just because she is Deaf,' spoke up Snow White.

'All deaf people deserve to die. She has no place in this world. And neither do you two!' Saying this, the queen took out a knife.

Just as the queen was moving towards Snow White, the rest of the little people arrived and captured her in a net meant for predators. The queen hung helplessly on a tree, crying for help.

'How did you know Shals and I were in distress?' signed Snow White.

'Your little birds!' smiled Tabish, pointing upwards. But they only saw Ruie up there. Snow White wondered where Bluie and Brownie were.

A few hours later, she saw Bluie and Brownie at her window. Behind them was her father. Her joy knew no bounds and she ran to embrace him.

Soon, the king, the little people and Snow White were all crammed into the hole-house, where he finally learnt the truth. He saw the queen wailing on a nearby tree. He wondered how he could have been so foolish all these years. A sharp pang of guilt and fury hit him, and he decided to take action against the whole situation once he was back at the palace. He thanked the men for shaping Snow White into a confident girl and told them humbly, 'The palace gates are always open to all of you.'

As Snow White was about to leave with her father, she signed, 'We meet thrice a week or I will get my birds to shit all over your hole-house.'

They all laughed and bid her farewell.

# Agal

## *By Dr P. Karkuzhali*

THE WALLS OF THE TWO-ROOMED HUT WERE BUILT OF baked bricks, roofed with wood and stringy bark, and floored with mud. A long wooden table and two armchairs made of bamboo sat in the right corner of the living room. A half-filled oil can, a pickle jar with cracks running around its top and an *anjarai petti* containing spices lined the wooden slab of the kitchen. Next to it, there was a tiny window streaming sunlight in every day. But now, it was almost dusk, and Agalvizhi was eagerly waiting for her husband's return.

'Amma is going to prepare kuzhipaniyaram for tonight. It's your appa's favourite dish. Be good until then.' With that, she laid down the child on the mat near the tiny window.

Agalvizhi took onions, green chillies and coconut from the basket kept below the wooden slab and reached for the *aruvamanai*. She sat comfortably on the floor with her right leg folded on the plank to which the curved blade was fastened and her left leg stretched out.

Her glass bangles jostled while she swiftly cut, onions and chillies against the blade. The air was thick with anticipation. Whenever she heard the crunch of footsteps on the gravel path, her heart skipped a beat. Before setting out the pan to fry the chopped onions in oil, she grated the coconut on the flat round top with sharp teeth.

Maaran entered the hut, calling out her name, 'Agalvizhi!' Overwhelmed with joy he said, 'Come, come here. See what I have brought for us.' Maaran was the king of Veera Puram. After his cousin Dhuruvan usurped the throne, Maaran was stripped of his noble status and was exiled to Madurai along with his family. They could not return home for fear of death. They had nothing left with them except their lives. Maaran, once the king, now had the responsibility to feed his wife Agalvizhi and his daughter Thendral. That morning, he had left home to look for a job.

'At last your appa has come.' Agalvizhi left the onions simmering on the stove, and they filled the small hut with a delicious aroma. She lifted the child off the mat, held her against her left hip and walked to the main door.

'What is it?' she asked with a smile.

'Find out for yourself. Here it is.' He placed the bundle near her.

Even before she could touch it, she sensed its bale smell.

'Quickly spin this bundle of straw into gold. With this we could soon get a new life. We could get back all that we lost.'

The smile on her face slowly faded. She stood still. Who would rescue her this time?

Her silence irritated him. 'What are you waiting for? You want me to beg you?'

'I know nothing of it,' Agalvizhi whispered the same thing she had told him when she met him for the first time in his palace. Would she be heard this time?

'You liar. Don't lie to me. How did you spin all the straw into gold then?'

'A little imp ...' She tried once again to explain what had really happened.

'Shut up. I have no time to listen to your wicked stories. Do what I say.'

'When did you ever have time to listen to me?' she muttered and moved towards the kitchen.

He rushed towards her, 'What? What did you say?'

His fingers burnt like fire. She freed her arms from his clutch at once and said, 'Nothing.'

'I heard you saying something. What? What is it?'

'I said, "I can't."'

'How dare you?'

'It's the truth.'

'What truth? Dirty beggar. Your appa exploited my innocence and deceitfully married you off to me.'

Her face turned red. 'Please ... don't bring my appa into this.'

Oh! I should stop talking about your beloved appa, is it? I will talk more and more about that foul-mouthed liar. He ruined my life.' The smell of charred onions spread around the room.

'It's not him, but you. Your avaricious desire ...' Her voice broke.

'What? Who ... Who is at fault? Me? Had he not bragged that you could spin straw into gold?'

'It was a metaphor! But masked by your greed for gold, it's you who is imprisoning me for the second time.'

'Stop. You useless woman. How dare you blame me!' He knocked the chairs to the floor. Startled by the loud crashing, her child stopped sucking her thumb and began crying.

'No, I've just said what had actually happened.'

'Yes. It's my fault. I should have chosen one of the princesses who sought me. My ill fate, my ill fate.' Kicking the chairs hard against the wall, Maaran left the house fuming. The wind stopped blowing and an ominous silence filled the room.

~

That night Agalvizhi could not sleep. Her face was stained with tears, and she wondered: 'Should a person with a disability be an extraordinary one to earn basic respect?'

Weighed down with grief, Agal recalled her parents' exhilaration when she was born. It was an unforgettable day. She was wrapped in a piece of cloth and shown to her parents. They were filled with joy when they held her in their hands.

'At last Goddess Sakthi, blessed us. Look how pretty she is! Our cute fairy!' her amma exclaimed with joy.

'She has come to rule the world. Look at her sparkling eyes. They shine with courage and wisdom.' With admiration, her appa took her in his hands and named her Agalvizhi.

At that moment, they did not know that God had other plans.

'Your child has a rare disorder and she may permanently lose her vision at any point of time.' The words of the physician made their blood run cold. They sobbed as they had never done before. It took at least a year for them to accept the scary reality that had befallen their child. Ever since then, they took good care of her. Their constant interactions with her made them understand her special needs. As she grew up, her vision gradually began to fade. Though they silently wept over her future at night, they never revealed their pain and insecurities to her. They found distinct ways to engage her in various activities. They stopped gesturing and initiated verbal interactions with her.

To enhance her learning ability, they set up a special play area for her in the corner of the courtyard. Her appa had carefully examined and bought appealing toys for Agal. Brightly coloured planks affixed with an array of wooden bird and animal images were placed in the multi-shelf cupboard against the wall. Wooden trays with raised edges containing kitchen play sets, alphabet blocks and different shapes were arranged neatly on the mud floor beneath the cupboard. Her amma would spend long hours sitting with her on the floor, encouraging Agal to identify the letters of the alphabet and shapes, name the animals and the birds, and differentiate between fruits and vegetables by touch, taste and smell. She would sing for her while feeding her. In the evenings, her appa would tell her stories, take her to the garden, prompt her to move around, make her observe the wind in the trees, the chirping birds and the buzzing bees. Together, they would explore different shapes and textures in nature. Agal enjoyed the playful interactions with her parents and relished the opportunities given to her to explore different sounds and environments. She joyfully moved her arms and legs in response to the rhythmic sounds of nature. Whenever her amma sang to her, she would smile in response to the music. They observed Agal playing with bells, tapping plates gently with spoons and singing short phrases of her amma's songs in perfect tune at the age of two.

Identifying her ability to sing, her appa decided to give her music lessons. Though he was earning only a meagre amount, he cut down all his expenses and spent everything that he had on imparting knowledge and musical skills to Agalvizhi. Whenever her athai came home to visit them, she would advise him with a stern face, 'Subhu, you are wasting your money on this girl. You are betting everything on this lame horse.'

He would gently explain, 'No akka. I am only investing in her future. The skills that she acquires today will empower her to live on her own later.'

Swirling her lips, Athai would retort sharply, 'Future? Whose future? Who will feed her just for her talent? This in no way is going to help her, and you will one day live on the stPritis if you spend everything on her.' No such forewarnings affected him. He took her to the famous Guru Ramanujam and pleaded with him to admit Agalvizhi as his pupil. Ramanujam observed her face quietly.

'Kanna, sing a song for me?' he asked.

'*Maargazhi thingal mathi niraintha nan naalaam* (The full moon day of the holy month of Maargazhi is here, bathing the auspicious day with moonlight)'—Agal's enthralling voice captivated his heart. After this, her music lessons began in a systematic manner.

~

It was on the first day of her music class that she met Raji. This was her first acquaintance with the outer world. Her appa made her sit with the other pupils and waited outside until her class got over. A sudden fear gripped her heart. She felt lost in the unfamiliar surroundings, but heavenly wafts from the sandalwood incense and the gentle fragrance of melting gheelamps infused the air of the pooja room and soothed her. 'Agalvizhi, come, let's sit together.' Raji's words comforted her. She took her by the hand. Until then, Raji had had no female companions in the music class. Quickly, they became friends.

Rajalakshmi was Guru Ramanujam's only granddaughter. Being an only child in her family, she was playful and pampered by everyone at home except Ramanujam. She was two years older than Agalvizhi and took pride in attending to her needs. 'Agal, you need water? Eat this fruit ... Shall I peel it for you?' Agalvizhi would say, 'No Akka. Thanks. Will eat after class, Akka.'

Impressed by Agalvizhi's keen interest in learning and her unfailing efforts, Guru Ramanujam focused his attention on her. He enthusiastically taught her all the subtleties of music. He would play the veena in admiration while she sang. Each time he praised her mastery over music, Raji grew envious of Agalvizhi. It was then that Agalvizhi began experiencing frequent hostilities from Raji. Whenever Guru Ramanujam was not around, Raji would pull

Agal's plaited hair, twist her ear or pinch her thigh to distract her while she was singing. Innocent Agalvizhi could not fathom Raji's evil intentions and would say, 'Akka, you have become playful these days!' Agalvizhi's passion for music made her excel in musical compositions even before she turned seven years old. Satisfied by her exceptional talent and hard work, Guru Ramanujam made arrangements for Agalvizhi's first Kacheri.

This news came to Raji as a thunderbolt. She threw tantrums at home that night.

'Raji, why are you so adamant? How long will you be like this? Come eat your dinner,' her amma begged her.

'Why should I eat? Nobody cares for me. All liars …'

Guru Ramanujam heard this as he was entering the house. 'What's the matter?'

'This one has become a big nuisance these days, appa. I have been begging her to eat for nearly an hour.'

'Rajalakshmi, come here. Why are you so reluctant to have your food? What is bothering you?'

'Am I not singing well, Thatha?'

'Who said so? This is what is troubling you? Yes. You sing well. Silly girl. Come. Let's eat.'

'Then why have you arranged for Agalvizhi's Kacheri and not mine?'

'Look here, Rajalakshmi, it is not possible for everyone to sing with perfection at this young age. She is blessed with an amazing talent. It's time that Agalvizhi should do her first Kacheri. As her guru, it's my duty to showcase her talent to the world.'

'But Thatha, am I not senior to her? I've been taking classes even before she joined. Shouldn't I be allowed to do my Kacheri before her?' She stamped her foot on the floor.

'Rajalakshmi, first stop comparing yourself with her. It's not about who is senior to whom. On the contrary, it is about who excels in the art.' Guru Ramanujam's voice had turned stern.

'Don't give me excuses. Just because she is blind you are favouring her and denying my rights to stage my Kacheri before her. Giving preference to my junior is nothing but a sheer insult to me.'

'Who taught you to talk like this? This attitude of yours is going to fetch no good for you. Go, eat first.' Guru Ramanujam dismissed her argument. Meanwhile, Raji made up her mind not to attend the Kacheri.

The next day, Agal was perplexed by her friend's absence. Later, through an overheard conversation between her appa and her guru, she discovered what had happened. She was pained and bewildered by Raji's behaviour. She felt the ground shake beneath her feet as she walked back home.

'Appa, am I not her friend? Doesn't she like me?'

'Yes. You are her friend and of course she likes you.'

'Then why did she not come for my Kacheri?'

'She was not well ...'

'Appa, please don't hide things from me. I heard everything.'

'Hmmm.'

'Tell me, appa. Why was she unhappy about my Kacheri?'

'See Agalvizhi, being an only child, adored by everyone, she's always got everything she wanted whether she deserved it or not.'

'Appa, I am her friend. Not her competitor. How could she be jealous of me?'

'Agalvizhi, such irrational feelings are everywhere. That is the world around you. You can't escape from such situations in your life.'

'But appa, I simply can't digest this. I feel betrayed.'

'I understand. Don't take it to heart. It will curb your growth.'

'I can't bear it, appa.'

'No. You must learn to come out of it. Remember, don't ever get struck by these things. Instead, be what you are and do what you can with confidence.'

In the present day, on this lovely night, remembering the story of Raji, Agalvizhi fell asleep.

~

It was half past six in the morning. The soft fragrance of blooming jasmines and the heavenly smell of vermilion wafted in the air. The chanting of mantras and the chiming of temple bells were overlaid by the delicate jingling of the *cilampu* worn by the temple-dancers. Though this backdrop charmed Agal's senses, it also caused intense pain.

Maaran had not returned home yet. Filled with anxiety, Agal went out and called out to Ponnamma atthai who lived next door. It was Ponnamma atthai who took good care of Agalvizhi and her child when they first reached Madurai. Forty-five-year-old Ponnamma atthai had been running a small eatery alone for years. She had lost her husband in the battlefield soon after their marriage, and she had no children of her own, so she treated Agalvizhi like a daughter. Having lost her own amma at a young age, Agalvizhi too relished the care and affection given to her.

'Atthai! Atthai!' she called out with a quivery voice.

'What's the matter, Agalvizhi? What happened?' Ponnamma atthai came rushing out.

'He has not come home yet.'

'Who? Maaran? He must have gone too far in search of a job. Might be held up somewhere. Don't worry. He'll be back soon.'

'No, atthai. He came home last night. Fought with me and stormed out angrily.'

'Fought with you? But for what?' Atthai asked, perplexed. So Agalvizhi narrated everything that happened the previous night.

'Hmmm. Situations like this make me question the existence of God. I don't know, Agal. Will he cast his eyes on your struggle? Let's see. But till then, you don't lose your hope.'

A week later, Ponnamma atthai met Maaran when she went to visit her sister in the next town.

'Thambi, please come home. Ever since you left home, Agalvizhi is sad and upset. I doubt whether she has had any sleep all these days.'

He immediately snubbed her saying, 'Enough of her. I can no longer live with a woman who cheated me.'

'Thambi, I think you have misunderstood Agalvizhi.'

'No, atthai. Only now I've got her right. Don't get carried away by her fake innocence. Do you think I am a fool to take all the burden on my shoulders and suffer alone? Tell her to look for some other fool who will serve her better for life. There is nothing left between us.'

'Thambi, It's quite normal to have fights and misunderstandings between couples. But don't let it ruin your relationship with her. Please don't make a quick decision when you are angry.'

'Only once, atthai, once I've made that mistake ... and now I am paying for it.'

'But Thambi ...'

'I've had enough of her. I've no second thoughts about my decision to leave her.' The fresh leaves crushed under his feet, as he walked away.

Agalvizhi's face grew dark when she heard this from Ponnamma atthai. The rustling winds outside her tiny hut slapped her face and arms. She tightened her saree against the wind.

'Nothing left between us! Perhaps I am not up to his level. Hmmm. What could a poor miller's daughter do for him?' Thendral crawled towards her with a whimper. She picked the child up and held her tightly against her bosom. 'How could he forget you? How could he simply walk out of his own child's life? Did he not think about you for even a moment!' She caressed her back and comforted the child.

She said to herself: 'It's time. I must go.'

~

It was five in the morning. The touch of the breeze, the humming of birds and the warmth of the morning twilight woke Agalvizhi up. She could sense a new life awaiting her. She had decided to step out to look for an opening to the big world.

Agal went to meet the temple *dharmagarthas* and wealthy patrons to seek opportunities to stage concerts at temple festivals. But she had a difficult time convincing them. Disability was seen as a sin.

'Amma, we greatly appreciate your mastery over the art of singing. But our hands are tied. We are not sure whether devotees and common folks would accept a disabled singer.' Invariably, this was the answer she received, but such responses failed to dampen her spirit. Days passed by. She did not give up. A few weeks later, the announcement of a music competition came to her as a blessing in disguise. As part of the birth celebrations of the prince, King Pandiya announced an open vocal music competition. 'The winner will receive one thousand gold coins.'

The voice of the *thandora* lingered in her ears. *Won't this be a great opportunity for me to display my talent to the world?* Agal thought to herself.

On the day of the competition, she took Thendral along with Ponnamma atthai and hurriedly boarded the cart. As the cart travelled through the crossroads of the bazaar, she heard the crackling footsteps of rushing pedestrians. The mesmerising fragrance of jasmine buds, the sweet aroma of fresh fruits from the shops, and the crispy *uzhundhu* vadai sizzling in hot oil at roadside eateries piqued her senses. As she got down from the cart and carefully stepped into the court, she was stopped by the gatekeeper.

'Who are you? What business do you have here?'

'I've come here to take part in the singing contest.'

'You! You are going to sing! What does a woman have to do with music? That too ...' The gatekeeper laughed. She stood silently.

'Where do you think you are?' thundered the gatekeeper. 'This is not the backyard of your house where you hum something while going about your household chores. It is King Pandiya's court. Great scholars, musicians and renowned poets have gathered here to judge the event.'

With a smile on her face, Agal firmly asked, 'Shall I go in?'

'Oh! You want to go in? Hmm. Go. They are going to have a good time with you.' His voice dripped with sarcasm.

As Agal walked in, an entrancing voice startled her. Her face grew pale. She stood still and felt a bitter taste in the back of her mouth.

'Agal? Agal, what happened?' Atthai sounded worried.

'This ... this voice sounds familiar to me, atthai.'

'Whose voice? The one who is singing?'

'Yes. The voice sounds familiar. It's been a really long time since I heard her voice. An old friend of mine ...'

'Agal, let's sit first. Come.' They went to the seats allotted for the singers.

'The competition began just a few minutes ago. We would have been on time if the gatekeeper had not delayed us.' Atthai tucked her saree tightly around her waist and sat next to her with Thendral on her lap.

Agal's stomach seemed to rise into her throat. It was the same feeling that she had experienced when she performed her first

Kacheri. Pulling herself together, she waited for her turn to come. Experienced singers were in line before her. Each one of them sang mellifluously. When her turn came, her heart thrummed. The chill breeze through the windows endearingly caressed her face and arms. The soft, spongy cushion beneath her comforted her as if she was sitting on her amma's lap. She sang a song she had written and composed in Charukesi.

> Silenced my voice with his threat—while testing thrice at his chamber.
> Mistook me for an alchemist—made me his queen.
> The tongue that praised me—treated me as a burden—as I could no longer fulfil his voracious desire.
> Stigma turned my dreams and dignity to ashes—though would I not rise from it?'

It was a song about her ordeal. She sang about her subjugation, stigmatization and her struggle for dignity. Her sad voice filled the interiors of the music chamber. The listeners were moved to tears. Like her first Kacheri, this too was a grand success. Impressed by her performance, the revered judges of the event unanimously announced Agalvizhi as the winner of the contest and presented her with one thousand gold coins. Greatly impressed by her talent in singing, King Pandiya offered her a permanent seat in the kingdom's prestigious art and literature academy. Hearing this, her heart yearned for her appa's presence. 'Had you been with me, wouldn't you be elated to hear this, appa? This privilege bestowed upon your daughter!' With immense respect and gratitude, she agreed to render her services towards the growth of art and literature in the Pandya kingdom.

～

Agalvizhi became the talk of the town for the next couple of weeks. The whole of Madurai was buzzing with the news of this new talented singer. Hearing this, Maaran returned home. At the time, Agalvizhi was busy packing her clothes to move to the trainer's quarters that had been offered to her.

'Agalvizhi, is what I heard true? You got one thousand gold coins as a gift from the king?' asked Maaran with a smile. Ever since that appalling night, she had not heard from him. She was dumbstruck when she heard his voice again. He walked up to her and shook her shoulder. 'Agal, don't you remember my voice? It's me. Maaran.' Annoyed by his touch, she instantly shoved his hands away. 'Yes. I do remember. What made you come here?'

'I know, dear. You are angry with me. I am at fault. I shouldn't have left you and our child to suffer alone in a new place. I have realized my mistake.' None of his sappy words softened her heart. She continued packing Thendral's clothes.

'Agal, now I am a changed man,' assured Maaran. 'Please believe me. Let's start afresh with the gift you have received from the king.'

The loud rattling noise of the cart advancing towards her house caught her attention.

'Agal, Agal, the cart is here.' Ponnamma atthai had come with the cart from the neighbourhood. 'Is everything ready? Shall we go?'

'Yes atthai!' said Agalvizhi in a cheery voice. Ponnamma atthai came inside to collect the luggage. The sight of Maaran struck her with astonishment. Agalvizhi noticed it by the sudden pause in atthai's stumbling footsteps. She handed over the bags to atthai and picked her child up from the cradle. 'Atthai, come let's go,' said Agalvizhi, moving towards the main door. Not knowing what to do, atthai accompanied her to the cart.

Never once had Maaran imagined that Agal would ignore him. He felt a bitter rage against her. 'No, it's not the right time,' he said to himself. He walked up to her again to mollify her. 'Agal, please listen to me. Your anger will only lead you to a wrong decision. It's not good for our child's future. You will certainly regret it later.' Hearing this, Agalvizhi got down from the cart , pulled out a pouch from her bag and handed it to Maaran. 'Here it is. The precious metal that you love the most. Take it. With this you can start a new life. A life that is free from all burdens. My appa's words have come true. I *can* spin straw into gold after all.'

# Quack

## by Niluka Gunawardena

THE RAIN HAD SUBSIDED, BUT THE CARNIVAL GROUND was still muddy, wet and cold and boggish. Di's feet were covered in a thick layer of dirt. She felt like she was slowly sinking into a pit of sludgy, dense gunk. The shackles that tied her to a post were firm and unforgiving. Any drastic movement would result in deep cuts on her left webbed foot. The cuts from her previous escape attempts were still fresh and raw. Just three days into life at the carnival, she had learnt to be still and obedient.

Di was glad that the long evening of curious and menacing visitors had come to an end. She was relieved that the glare of the distorting carnival lights flickering and illuminating the 'Marvellous Oddities' tent had gone to sleep for the night. She was glad that she was no longer drowning in the cacophony of garbled sounds.

The carnival was a place of dizzying sounds. The sound of the little three-eyed piglet in the pen next to her squealing and crying out in distress. The sound of children jeering at the Siamese Sisters—

124

conjoined cats who drew large numbers of crowds. The terrifying, strange and foreboding sounds made by 'The Monstrosity' that was kept at the back of the tent. Di was afraid of the monstrosity although she had never seen it. She had heard children cry out in fear and disgust when they approached it. That was enough to make Di's blood curdle. Di had also seen glimpses of the albino bear when she was first brought into the tent. He was a large, hulking creature kept in a small, constricted cage. Di didn't hear a sound from him. She wondered how such an imposing creature could be quieter than a mouse.

She knew that there were many other creatures in the tent based on the strange and 'odd' noises that they made. They were all afraid of each other in one way or another. After all, the children who saw them would scrunch their faces in disgust and fear, and the little kids would hide behind their parents and sometimes shriek. Surely, they must all be horrible and frightening in their cages, pens and shackles—so they thought of themselves and each other as monstrous.

Throughout the day and well into the night, you could hear the constant, lulling noise of the carousel in front of the 'Marvellous Oddities' tent. The never-ending jolly tune of the rotating merry-go-round sounded ominous and chilling to Di. Most of the children who went for a ride on the carrousel ended up coming to Di's tent. That tune made Di feel sick in the stomach. But it had stopped—for now.

Di was glad for the respite and the darkness that was more in keeping with her mood and internal weather than the bright, harsh lights that would stun anyone who looked at them for too long. The only sounds she heard were the occasional groans and moans from the direction of 'The Monstrosity'. Part of her was somewhat glad that they were all in cages. At least they were safe from each other!

Every night brought a few hours of quiet. And every night, on the wings of stillness and darkness, would come memories of her past. These memories led Di back to a place of warmth, comfort, love and acceptance. The cloak of slumber took Di back to the folds of her mother's wings. Oh, how she ached for that warmth and ease—no care in the world, just snuggling in the fluffy, gentle, feathery bosom of her mother. But that was a long time ago ...

~

Di was the youngest among three little ducklings. While Di's brother and sister had beautiful, fluffy, pastel-yellow feathers, Di had a sparse and prickly grey exterior. The beaks of her siblings were tangerine orange and Di's was black like burnt charcoal. When she was very young, Di had no idea that she looked any different from her siblings. She thought that someday they would all become beautiful and elegant ducks like their mother. Di's mother never did or said anything that made her feel different. She cared for all three of her younglings with great love and affection.

Di's first month of life was blissful. She and her siblings lived in a cosy nest on the luscious banks of an effervescent pond. She didn't go out of her nest in that first month—she had no reason to do so. Her mum would bring worms, insects and lovely little treats for her little ducklings every few hours.

Di loved to sing chirpy little songs with her brother and sister. Her sister Sally, the eldest, would always sing the lead, and her brother Aaron would beatbox. Di was asked to sing the chorus parts, but she didn't mind. She was happy to be part of the family singing troupe. Their mother, who had the most soothing voice, told them the story of the Von Flap family, a large family of singing ducks in Austria. Di and her siblings were inspired by this story and called themselves the Von Quacks. Their mother had also told them wonderful stories about their grandfather Harold, who had been the birdsong conductor of Waverly Pond. Sally wanted to follow in his footsteps. Aaron was a more mischievous sort and thought himself very cool, being the beatboxer in the family.

As the three little ducklings grew, he started calling Di 'Blacky' because she was darker than the rest of her family. Their mother said that sometimes it took time for little ducklings to get the lemony yellow coloured feathers that Sally and Aaron had. She often told all three of her little ducklings that they were very beautiful. Di was proud to be her mother's beautiful little duckling.

The three ducklings loved to listen to their mother's stories about the outside world—the world they sang about in their chirpy songs. Di could hear the gurgling of the water and the sound of other ducks from afar. She wondered what the world outside looked like. She did not have to wonder for long. Soon the time came for Di and her siblings to learn how to be ducks and to venture outside the nest. The ducklings jumped around in great anticipation and excitement. 'Yay! We are going on an adventure!' chirped Aaron while Sally did a little jig of joy. Little Di tried to keep up with the jubilant song and dance of her brother and sister.

Mother then told them in a firm tone: 'Ducklings! The first big lesson in being a duck is discipline and conformity. You need to learn how to follow your leader, you need to learn to fit in to your flock, you need to learn to swim and fly in formation. You can't just jump about. Now, let's stand in formation. One duckling behind the other—the eldest in front—the youngest at the back. For now, I am your leader, so you need to follow me. No diversions or distractions!'

The three ducklings got in line as instructed by their mother, with Di as the youngest at the very end of the line. Order, rank, duty and fitting in—these values were very important to ducks, especially the ducks of Waverly Pond, where Di and her siblings were born.

Nighttime at the carnival took Di back to that day: waddling behind her mother and siblings, making her way through the tall, luscious grass to the banks of beautiful Waverly Pond. Di marvelled at the big, blue, open sky. She saw a flock of ducks in flight and thought, *Wow! I would love to fly like that one day.* She loved the feel of the tall grass against her fluffy feathers. It was a little ticklish but nice. She loved the warmth of the sun on her face and how the pond glistened in the golden morning light. It was a very happy day for the three little ducklings.

Di looked around and saw other clusters of ducklings with their mothers. This was the first time the new little ducklings of Waverly pond were entering the Pond. It was an important day for everyone.

~

'Follow me, little ducklings,' said Di's mum as she gently glided into the water. She made it look so easy. 'Come, little ducklings,' she said to her children. With some hesitation, her big sister followed suit. Di felt queasy in the pit of her stomach but she remembered what her mother said about following the leader and sticking to formation. It was Aaron's turn. He let out a little squeal as he got into the water and was met with a quick disapproving glance by his mother. Di knew that look. This was not the time to be scared or fool around. She held her breath and stepped into the water after her brother. The water was cold. It made Di feel awake and alert. She was proud to follow her mother and siblings in line formation. She looked at the other ducklings who were also swimming behind their mothers. They looked beautiful!

*We must look beautiful too*, thought Di. *How wonderful it is to swim together. This must be what it's like to be a proper duck.*

Di's mother gently guided them around the shallower waters of the pond where the other little ducklings and their mothers were.

'Ugly duckling, ugly duckling,' shouted some ducklings from the banks. They looked a bit older than the little ducks in the pond. They were looking in Di's direction and laughing.

'Who could this ugly duckling be?' Di wondered.

Just then another mother duck came to Di's mum and asked in a hushed tone, 'Oh what an ugly little duckling you have! Whatever is the matter with her? Is she sick?'

'No, she is fine,' said Di's mother. 'She was just born this way.'

The other mother duck looked at Di with disgust.

'Oh no! She is talking about me!' Suddenly it dawned upon Di that many ducks and ducklings were gawking and staring at her. She had been so preoccupied with following her mother that she had not noticed the stares.

*Oh no! Oh mummy! Oh no! Oh no!* Di thought. She wanted to hide under her mother's wing but remembered what she had been told about staying in formation, and stayed behind her older sister and brother. At that moment, she looked at the water and saw her reflection—her own image and form—for the first time in her life. Dark charcoal beak; spikey, sooty, feathers with brownish patches; tawny, twiggish brown webbed feet. 'Oh no—those poo-coloured patches … It's me! The youngling ducks are laughing at me!' Di felt stunned. She wanted the pond to swallow her up so that she could disappear forever. But no, there she was, and there her mother was—out in the open, starred at, jeered at. As if reading her mind, Aaron whispered, 'It's okay, Blacky, you are going to be okay.' He was just trying to protect his little sister, but the only thing that struck Di was 'Blacky'—black equals ugly!

Di could see the older ducks pointing to her family and whispering. Some of the little ducklings, emboldened by the jeers of the teenage ducks, started taunting Di. They shouted hurtful things that made Di feel very bad and very small.

'That's enough for today,' said Di's mother and took the ducklings home. The walk home felt heavy and terrible for everyone, especially Di. It was supposed to be a day of fun and adventure but instead it had ended up being a day of fear and shame for their family. Di wanted so desperately to tell her mother how sorry she was, but her mother didn't look back. She just kept walking, moving forward in formation as she had been taught by those before her. 'When in trouble, never give up, and never look back,' she had been told by grandpa duck Harold when she was a wee duckling. She wanted so badly to protect her ducklings, to protect little Di, but she didn't know how, at least not at that moment. She had faced her fair share of pain and rejection and knew there would be challenges the day Di was born, but she didn't think it would be this bad. Sally could sense her mother's unspoken sorrow, so she tried to be strong for her family—after all, she was the eldest. Di started whimpering and sobbing.

'Hold on to my tail, Blacky,' said Aaron. While Di hated the name 'Blacky', now more than ever, she was happy to hold on to Aaron's tail, in case she got lost in the whirlwind of crushing pain. Aaron wanted to make sure Di was okay, but he also felt angry inside. He really wanted to play with the other ducklings, to be a 'cool duck' but now they had to go hide at home because of Di. He felt very conflicted inside, but he wasn't going to abandon his baby sister.

～

That evening, Di's uncle Ronald, her mother's brother, came to visit them. Ronald had visited them twice before and had brought tasty worms for the children. This time, Ronald didn't bring any worms for the children; he didn't even gPriti them. He asked his sister to step out of the nest to talk outside. The adults spoke in hushed voices, but Di was able to eavesdrop. She heard bits and pieces of the conversation.

'I told you not to take her out, but you never listen do you?' said Ronald in a stern voice. 'You ended up a single mother with an abnormal child because of your own foolishness. Do you ever think about us—about our reputation and honour?

'We are ducks of Waverly Pond! You don't want the two good ones to suffer just because of the ugly one. Weaklings are left outside for the vultures. Nature takes care of them. That's how things are done here. You have brought great shame on our family!'

'The ugly one'—that reference pierced Di's little heart, over and over again—'the ugly one'.

That night, Di snuggled into the folds of her mother's wings with Sally and Aaron on either side. She had never felt so horrible, bad and unwanted in her short life. She wanted to disappear. She was not supposed to be here. She felt her mother heaving slightly. Di half-opened her eyes to see silent tears rolling down her cheeks.

At that moment, Di wished her mother would leave her out for the vultures like her uncle had advised. But she didn't do it. The next morning her mother woke the ducklings up with a beautiful song.

'Three little ducks that I once knew—a big one, a fluffy one and a tiny one too. The one little duck with a feather on her back—she led the others with a quack, quack, quack.'

Di basked in the comfort of her mother's voice. It was like a balm for her aching heart. 'Little Di, it is best you stay at home and rest today,' said her mother. 'Come, Sally and Aaron, let's get in formation.' Sally gave Di a look—a look of both sadness and dismay. 'Don't worry Di, we will bring you yummy worms to eat when we come back.' She gave Di a quick peck on the cheek on her way out. Aaron was lost in his own little world and didn't think much about leaving Di—at least not at that moment. And Di's mother went out with her brother and sister, leaving Di behind.

A little while later, she heard a big din outside the nest.

'Ugly duckling, ugly duckling, come out and play!'

It was the gang of teenage ducks from the day before. They had figured out that Di was home alone. Di was as quiet as she could be. Then one of the teenage ducks said, 'Your mother is such a loser for giving birth to an ugly thing like you.' The teenagers started laughing, saying, 'Your mum is a loser!' They had hit Di where it hurt the most. She felt enraged! She could not bear to hear the young ducks mocking and ridiculing her mother any longer. Without thinking, she stepped out of the nest and shouted, 'Don't you dare say anything about my mother!'

She instantly regretted coming out. The young ducks were much bigger than her. 'Puny little ugly duck,' said one of the bigger ones. 'Maybe we should do your mother a favour and get rid of you.'

'Don't you think that's a good idea, little ugly duckling?' said another. Those words pierced through Di's heart like a poisoned arrow. Yes, she wished they would get rid of her. Di started crying, feeling utterly unwanted. 'Oh poor little ugly duckling,' said one of the ducks mockingly. Then, the young ducks formed a circle around her and started pushing her from one duck to another, all the while heckling, jeering and taunting.

Di felt numb and cold. She could not feel her body as the young ducks kept passing her around like she was a rag doll. She fell down in the middle of the circle. Then the oldest of the lot picked her up. 'Ugly ducklings like you don't belong in Waverly Pond. You are a shame to our pond, you are a shame to your family, you are a shame to your mother. Look at how ugly you are! You are like a half-baked cookie! How can you even call yourself a duck?'

All the ducks started laughing. They thought it was hilarious. 'Run, little ugly duckling. Run, run and never come back!' Di picked herself up with great effort and ran. She ran and ran and ran and never looked back.

~

Di did not know where she was going. She ran aimlessly as far away as she could from her mother, her brother, her sister, her uncle and Waverly Pond. The darkness of night fell upon her and she finally crashed into a heap of ugliness under a shrub, exhausted. Di vaguely registered endless fields of wheat interspersed with farmhouses. She was on the outskirts of a farming community. She did not have the energy to notice much else. Every inch of her tiny body was wracked with pain. Far more acute than the physical pain was the gut-wrenching sense of isolation that plagued her heart.

It was mid-morning when Di opened her eyes. She had survived the night. She slowly made her way to the nearest farmhouse, parched and dehydrated. There was a bowl of water outside the farmhouse. Di took some sips when a shrill voice stopped her in her tracks.

'Who dares drink my water? Get away, you vile and unsightly creature!'

Di saw a very angry-looking tabby cat walking towards her. 'I am so sorry,' said Di. At that moment, the enormity of her banishment struck her like a thunderbolt. The little ugly duckling started crying and wailing, 'I'm sorry, I'm sorry, I'm sorry!'

This caught the tabby cat off guard. She didn't think the small creature would get so upset. She just sat there watching the duckling cry. She didn't know how to deal with small creatures, especially ones so pitiful. She was used to being the lady of the manor, Farmer Johnson's beloved feline companion. After a few moments, she moved closer to the sobbing creature. 'Now, now, this is not something to get so upset about. I don't share my water with anyone usually.'

Di kept sobbing and saying, 'I am sorry.'

A large, fluffy dog arrived. He was Farmer Johnson's sheepdog. 'What's going on here?' he said.

'I am so sorry for everything,' Di told the big dog.

'You look like you haven't eaten in days, little one,' he said.

'Come, I will take you to the chickens. They are the only birds we have around here. Stop crying now and come with me.'

Di looked at the sheepdog with the big, kind eyes. Kindness—something that reminded Di of her mother. She reluctantly followed him to the pen where the chickens were.

'Chickens, I found a lost one, an orphan. It looks like a bird of some sort so I brought it here.'

The chickens gathered around to inspect the new little creature. 'Is it really a bird?' said one. 'What is it? What are you?' asked another.

She wanted to say that she was a duckling but then she remembered what the teenage ducks had told her—that someone as ugly as her could never be a duck. So, she kept quiet. She did not know what she was. She just knew that she was ugly ...

'Have compassion for the creature,' said the big dog with the kind eyes. 'It doesn't say much, this critter, but it looks starved and parched. Maybe you can share your chicken feed and water with it?'

The chickens on Farmer Johnson's farm were divided on the matter. An older hen said, 'This creature looks ugly! What if it is sick? We will all get contaminated and die!' Several others agreed, but a few of the younger chickens were more willing to give Di a chance. By now, Di had become very frightened of younglings, teenagers—those who were no longer little ones but still not big ones.

'Shh it's okay, it's okay,' said one of the youngling chickens. 'We are the only birds around here and the older birds are very suspicious of any others who do not look like them. I think they would be more accepting if you looked more like us.'

'I have an idea,' said another youngling bird. 'Come with me!' The younglings took Di into the farmhouse. There was a big mound of flour on the floor. 'Now jump in this mound of flour,' said the youngling chicken. Di septically and hesitantly did as she was told. 'See, now you are white. You look a bit more like us. A bit like a chicken.'

Just as the youngling chickens had said, the others were more willing to let Di hang around now that she looked more like them. She was never fully a chicken though—so she had to eat and drink only after all the others had finished, living off the scraps of others. Farmhouses, like ponds, had their own hierarchies and Di pretty much was on the same rung as the mice!

Di bathed in flour every morning to pass as a chicken. The main thing was to maintain the peace and order of things. She had learnt that lesson in no uncertain terms on the day that she was banished from Waverly Pond. As a few months passed, Di's feathers started turning whiter and lighter on their own.

*Maybe I am a chicken after all*, thought Di. The big old sheepdog who had been so kind to her the day she arrived at the farm continued to watch out for her from a distance. He didn't say much to her, but he was one of the most senior and most respected figures of the farmhouse and his unspoken protection of Di meant that no one would outwardly harm her. The name 'ugly' stuck even at the farm, but she was not bullied like she was at Waverly Pond. In some sense, she belonged to the farm community as long as she lay low and refrained from drawing too much attention to herself.

Her body was growing and changing with the passage of time, and she started acquiring some new features. Dark red warts appeared on her beak. They slowly started spreading to her face. At first, she was able to hide the red warts with her flour bath, but as she grew older, the warts became redder and more prominent. Her body was becoming fuller and more 'bird-like', but her facial transformation began alarming the others. After one point, half of her face was covered in cherry red wattles.

Then it came—the bird flu that affected poultry farms across the country. Farmer Johnson's birds were not spared. Suddenly, young and fit chickens started to die. Some among them were the younglings who had lobbied to take Di into the farmhouse community. Some older hens could not stop wondering if it was indeed the ugly bird that had brought this wave of misfortune to their community. One day, they had a meeting of elders. The kind sheepdog and Farmer Johnson's tabby cat were also present. A chicken elder pointed out how more and more chickens were dying as more and more of Di's face got 'disfigured' with red warts and wattles.

'There is obviously a relationship between the two,' said the elder. 'We always knew she would be a source of contamination and contagion, and now youngsters in our community are paying with their lives because we decided to keep this ugly thing on our farm.' As kind as the big, brown-eyed sheepdog was, he was also not sure if Di had anything to do with this sudden wave of illness and disease. What if it *was* Di who was making the others sick? How could he take a chance and jeopardize the lives of the other chickens on his farm?

That night, the old sheepdog came up to Di and sat next to her. He looked at her with eyes full of tenderness and concern. 'My dear, you are indeed an unusual and curious creature. My heart reached out for you when you came here as a wee little one. But you have heard the talk about your condition and the sickness that is spreading through this farm, haven't you? I am sorry, my dear, but I can't hold the fort for you any longer. We had a meeting of elders. It was decided that you should leave the farm at daybreak tomorrow.'

*The story of my life*, thought Di as she silently bowed to the big sheepdog in agreement. As her heart wailed, not a tear fell from her eyes. She felt hollow and empty—as if her tears had dried out.

The next day, Di stoically left the farmhouse before any of the other animals woke up. She didn't say goodbye. She just disappeared. That was the only thing she seemed to be good at. Di wandered back to the outskirts of the farming community—back to the shrubs she had hidden under as a frightened little ugly duckling. Her mind was heavy with a fog of rejection and exclusion. She felt scattered and internally torn. Suddenly, she felt a sharp pain sear through her webbed foot. She was pulled up with a jolt and she passed out immediately. Di had fallen into a hunter's trap. When she came about, she was in a sack!

'I thought this ugly bird would be a good addition to your freak show,' said a man with a gruff voice. That is how Di ended up in Mister's 'Marvellous Oddities' tent.

~

Di woke up with a start. Mister was shouting 'Wakey, wakey, creatures!' hitting the bars of the cages that housed his prized exhibits. Mister's 'Marvellous Oddities' tent was part of a travelling circus. That morning, the oddity cages were all being packed into a rusty old train carriage for the trip north to Canada. For the first time, Di came face to face with the other 'freaks' in the show. The big albino bear in the small cage was bent over and crouched, looking belittled and broken. He turned away from the sunlight and covered his face with his big paws. Di could not help but wonder what a majestic creature he must have been before he was entrapped by Mister. Di saw the three-eyed little piglet in a small cage. While it was ugly in standard terms, there was something sweet and endearing about the little creature. Watching its childish antics, Di felt a sliver of affection and warmth in her bones and a sense of affinity crept into her heart. Perhaps this is how the sheepdog felt on the day she arrived at Farmer Jonhson's farmhouse as a little ugly duckling. The piglet looked frightened, lonely and cold.

'What is your name, dear one? My name is Di.' The little three-eyed piglet looked up at Di in surprise. No one had spoken to him that way since he had been separated from his mother several weeks ago.

'Oh,' whimpered the little piglet, 'please, don't hit me.' The piglet was still scarred by the memories of his mother being bludgeoned to death for her meat before he was given away to Mister for the oddities tent. He recoiled every time someone tried to touch him. Almost all the exhibits in Mister's oddities tent carried a deep sense of trauma.

'I would never hit you, little piglet,' said Di. She was surprised that she still had some tenderness inside her. Here was this tiny frightened creature invoking feelings that she had not felt in a very long time. Di shared her story with the little piglet who began to feel a bit safer in her presence, knowing that she too had been little and scared at one point. The piglet confessed that he didn't know his name. His mother had called him Baby and Mister had labelled his exhibit at the oddities tent 'Cyclops', but he wasn't sure if that was his name.

'What would you like to be called?' asked Di.

The piglet thought for some time and said, 'Can you please call me Baby?'

'Of course, I will,' said Di. Di finally had a friend in Baby, someone to call her own.

That night, Mister came to the train carriage to check on his oddities. He shone his light into each of the cages, enabling Di to get a better look at the others in the freak show. She was most curious about 'The Monstrosity' that made such a frightful sound.

She expected to see a big, hulking creature. Instead, she saw a being that looked a bit like a deer with a twisted body and a scarred face. There was a great depth of pain in the creature's eyes. She did not expect that at all. Instead of the fear that had earlier clouded her perception of 'The Monstrosity', a sense of warmth and connection arose within her. It was as if this journey had opened up a part of her that she didn't think existed ever since she ran away from Waverly Pond.

The next day, when Mister came to check on his oddities in the train carriage, Di carefully followed his torchlight. The other animals did not seem keen to look at each other but Di was riveted. Having realized how wrong she had been about 'The Monstrosity', Di was eager to see the rest of the freaks for who they were. Mister's torch shone on a big bottle, inside of which there was a rose-pink snake who was quite beautiful in its own way. Next, the light fell on a jaguar-like creature with dark, scaly, fishy skin. Then there was a bison with mangled horns. Mister called it 'The Centaur'. There was a large glass container full of bee-like creatures with a label reading 'murder hornets'. There was a mammoth creature that appeared to be a hybrid between a crocodile and a lizard. And there was a very hairy monkey with dreadlocks!

'What fascinating creatures,' thought Di. It was hard to clearly identify the animals at the back of the train carriage but Di did get glimpses of their eyes. Most of them were wellsprings of sadness—a commonality that registered in Di's heart, slowly replacing her fear and foreboding with a sense of kinship. As Di pondered on the nature of the freaks in Mister's tent, Baby, the three-eyed piglet, called out to Di from the adjoining cage.

'Di, please sing me a song. I can't fall asleep.'

Di recalled the song that her mother had sung on the day she ran away from Waverly Pond—the song about the three little ducklings who went 'quack quack quack'. She sang in a gentle and soothing voice until the little piglet fell asleep.

~

It was the dead of the night. Di had fallen asleep with these new realizations slowly dawning on her. Suddenly there was a big jolt, and the train came to a screeching halt! An obstacle on the track had derailed the train and the train carriage that the oddities were perilously tilted towards a deep valley. All the cages started crashing into each other and sliding to one side of the carriage. The carriage soon broke off from the rest of the train and fell down the slope towards the valley. There was a great din and consternation among the creatures. Gawking, roaring, crying, whimpering, moaning, growling, hissing, squealing, snapping, crashing, rattling, breaking. The carriage flipped twice and finally landed in the valley. The backdoor to the carriage had flung open upon impact and some of the cages had been damaged enough for the creatures that inhabited them to crawl out. Some of them were badly injured. The Siamese Sisters were entirely crushed under a cage—there was blood splattered all over. Baby cried out in fear and alarm. It was still very dark so Di found it difficult to gauge the full extent of the damage. Di started inching towards Baby's cries and suddenly realized that she could move freely. The chain that tied her to a post had snapped when the train carriage tumbled down to the valley.

Suddenly it dawned upon her: 'I am free!' Di saw that some other freaks had also managed to get out or fall out of their cages. The carriage door was open—there was nothing to stop them from running away!

'I must find Baby,' thought Di as she searched the carriage in the dark to find him. 'I am coming for you, Baby!' said Di as she tried to separate Baby's voice from the moans and groans of the others.

'Mommy, Mommy!' cried Baby. Finally, she found him, huddled in a corner with an injured foot.

'It's okay, Baby—I am here. It's okay,' said Di. 'We are going to get out of here.'

Baby's cage door was fairly intact and his foot was injured, so it was extremely painful for him to walk. 'Please, somebody help me,' cried Di.

She went to the big, hulking albino bear. 'Please, Sir, help me get Baby out of his cage,' she pleaded with him, but the albino bear remained hunched and silent. His cage door was wide open but he did not seem to realize that he could actually leave his cage. In fact, many of the animals showed no interest in venturing out of the known and familiar confines of the train carriage and the freak show. It was as if they no longer knew how to be free!

Di implored the albino bear several times, but to no avail. She frantically looked around to find a makeshift tool to break open Baby's cage door. She had to get Baby out before Mister and the rest of the circus crew came to get them. Suddenly and unexpectedly, the hairy monkey with dreadlocks came to Di with an iron bar and said, 'Name is Janice. Let's get this kid out of here.' Di and Janice pulled and heaved until finally, they were able to yank open the door to Baby's cage. Di rushed in to comfort Baby who was shivering. Di realized that they were running against time.

'We need to get out of here,' she told Janice. 'Get the others together.' While Janice tried to encourage the other freaks to leave the carriage, Di tended to Baby with deep love and affection. 'Come on, little one, get on my back,' she said while softly singing the 'three little ducks' song.

With Baby on her back, Di walked to the entrance of the train carriage and turned to speak to the others. 'Friends, we have been prisoners of this freak show, prisoners of exclusion, prisoners of self-loathing and resignation for far too long. Now is our time, now is the time to break free and start a new life together. Let us escape while we can!'

A few of the animals heeded Di's plea, but most of them remained unmoved.

'The world outside is cruel, harsh and unforgiving,' said the Centaur. 'They will never accept us. It is better for us to stay here in the circus. Surely Mister will come to rescue us.'

A few other freaks also voiced their agreement. 'Why should we go back to a world where we don't belong!' said the six-limbed deer.

Di started noticing torchlights from afar. 'They are coming to get us! We need to escape, now!'

Baby was slumped on Di's back. Janice and, surprisingly, 'The Monstrosity' followed suit. Di thought she saw the pink snake slither out of the carriage as well.

They ran as fast as they could. It was something that Di had mastered—running away, but this time it felt less like running away and more like running towards something. For the first time she was not running alone, she was running with friends, and this realization filled her with a renewed sense of strength and purpose. The freaks followed the river and ran along the valley into the thick of the forest. At daybreak, they came to a clearing with a large, effervescent pond—much like Waverly Pond. As if reading her mind, Janice said, 'Let's camp here for a bit and rest. I will see if I can find food for us.' 'The Monstrosity' didn't say much and wandered off to the pond to have a drink of water. It would be some time before 'The Monstrosity' opened up to the others. Baby had fallen asleep. Di tucked him into a patch of tall grass and ventured towards the pond. To her great surprise, Di saw a flock of very ugly birds—birds that looked a lot like her! Sooty feathers with a blackish splattering, faces covered in blood-red wattles and dark webbed feet. Who were these ugly birds?

Suddenly she heard a shrill voice say, 'Well, hello beautiful! First time seeing you here!' She turned towards the voice and saw a duck uglier than her!

'Who are you?' asked Di in shock and amazement.

'My name's Maureen,' said the ugly duck. 'We come here every summer from Mexico.'

'Mexico!' Di said in surprise. 'Isn't that a long way from here?'

'It sure is, love. We make a long trip here every year. It is a family tradition. You see, we are the Moscovy clan.'

Di simply could not believe her eyes—a large, loud, graceless clan of ugly ducks—just like her!

'You should join us on our flight back to Mexico,' said Maureen.

'Thanks, but I need to take care of my family,' said Di, glancing over at Baby, who was tucked away in the tall grass.

Just then Janice turned up and said, 'Well I can't believe my eyes! It is a whole nation of uglies like you!'

Di and Maureen laughed. 'Don't be so quick to judge,' said Maureen. 'We are the Moscovy clan of Mexico! And aren't you quite an unsightly-looking thing yourself,' she said in jest.

It was a comforting feeling—laughing at oneself—laughing at each other—a gathering of freaks and uglies. Di felt like there was some grace to it all. For the first time in her life, she felt comfortable in her own ugly skin. And it felt so good!

That evening, Di, Baby, Janice and Rose, the pink snake, joined the Moscovy ducks for their evening song. 'The Monstrosity' was not ready to mingle yet. Tears ran down Di's eyes as she remembered singing with Sally, Aaron and her mother as a baby duck. She wondered if Sally had indeed become the conductor of Waverly Pond. She wondered if her mother, brother and sister ever thought of her and missed her. Perhaps one day she would see them again—only time would tell. Di looked around at her new family and sang her heart out that evening, feeling a deep sense of belonging and fraternity—something she had not felt in the longest time. That evening, while tucking Baby to sleep, Di assured him that he would be okay. In her heart of hearts, Di knew that she would be okay too.

So begins the story of Di's life as a 'freedom fighter' and the adventures of her new-found family. How a Muscovy duckling ended up in Waverly Pond remains a mystery though!

# Maryam and the Moon Angel

## *by Sanchita*

ONE EVENING, AS THE SKY TURNED FROM ORANGE TO red, Zaheda came to the terrace to check on what Maryam was doing. Maryam spent a lot of time on the terrace. She had her own corner where she sat on a wooden chair next to the yellow and orange marigold flowers Zaheda had planted. There, she would talk to Moon Angel.

'Maryam, O Maryam,' Zaheda called her daughter while climbing up the stairs. With her face resting on her palm, Maryam kept watching the children playing on the other terraces, running, jumping over walls, panting, stopping to catch their breath. Zaheda gave her a marigold but Maryam did not take it. Yusuf and Zoya were yelling and screaming.

'Yay. No, I caught you. Tara, you tell me—didn't I catch him just now?'

'When?'

'Oh, right here. Just now. Didn't you see? Why are you so blind?' Yusuf asked.

145

All the children started laughing. *Tara is not blind. Why do they talk like that! As if it were a bad thing to be blind*, Maryam thought.

'Maryam, Maryam.' Zaheda tapped on her daughter's arm. 'What happened?'

'I do not want to play with them,' Maryam said. 'They are not good kids. None of them are my friends. When they laugh while playing, it feels like they are making fun of me.'

'Did anyone say something to you?' Zaheda asked. 'Maryam, O Maryam.'

'Hmm.' Maryam, still looking down, nodded.

'What did they say, Maryam?' Zaheda asked, placing her hand below Maryam's chin.

'I asked them if I could play. They started laughing at me.' Saying this, Maryam hugged Zaheda and started to cry. Zaheda held her tightly in her arms as she wiped Maryam's tears and kissed her head.

~

The only game Maryam gets to play is with the moon. Every day, she sits in her corner and travels to her own world—a world of dreams where she can fly and reach the moon. She, in fact, talks to the moon every night. She calls him Moon Angel.

'Ammi, I was on this big tower where Zulfia Khala went.'

'Which big tower?'

'Where Zulfia Khala went.'

'In Dubai?'

'Yes, yes. In Dubai. That's where I went. I waved at my Moon Angel. You know how big Moon Angel looked from there? It was as big as the very big white round crochet tablecloth you made at Haveli. It was that big.' Maryam showed her mother with both her arms, spreading them as far as she could.

'What did he say?' Zaheda asked.

'Who, Moon Angel? Nothing. He was very happy to see me standing so close to him.'

Zaheda laughed. Maryam's stories reminded her of her own childhood.

'You know what I did there?' Maryam continued. 'I went up to the sky like a rocket, then dove back onto the road like a superhero. Ammi, I also stopped a child from running in front of a car. I'll go there one day to see what is there, what everyone talks about after they come back from Dubai.'

Maryam does not remember how it happened. Occasionally, she wishes she could have stopped it but she hadn't been old enough at the time it happened. 'Ammi, Ammi! What happened?' she would sometimes ask Zaheda.

'When?'

'What happened to my leg, Ammi?'

'What happened to your leg? You have two legs just like everybody else does!'

But she was not like everybody else. *Why else wouldn't other children play with me?* she would often wonder. Maryam wanted to play with other children, run around like a superhero with a cape, her hands stretched out behind her. Nobody would have been able to catch her ever. If it had not happened, her mother would not have to drop her to school every day. She could have gone with the other children in the neighbourhood.

～

One day, Maryam was sitting in her classroom, her seat next to the window. She would often look outside, watching people's legs as they walked by. Or she would stare at the sky, feeling the breeze of the wind on her arms. She would close her eyes as she swayed with any bird she could lay her eyes on. Mostly it was a kite, a crow or a pigeon. Every time a pigeon came and sat on the windowsill, she would turn her head and look into its eyes and smile. The pigeon would also stare back, tilting its neck a little to the left, then further left to look closer into Maryam's eyes, 'Gutar gu … gutar gu …'

Maryam understood every word, both spoken and unspoken. She would answer every question Pigeon had for her.

'Ammi, Pigeon comes to meet me every day. He talks to me,' she would later tell Zaheda.

That day was no different. Pigeon had come to meet her. Maryam was smiling, looking at Pigeon's eye without blinking. Suddenly, she could feel Sara's hand on her shoulder. 'Maryam! Uff …'

'What happened?' Maryam asked, turning towards Sara.

'Can't you hear? Mandira Ma'am has been calling you.'

'Oh no …' Maryam stood up with her head down.

'What on earth were you doing? Do you know how many times I called your name?' Mrs Mandira Bose said.

Maryam, very softly biting her lower lip, said, 'Sorry, Ma'am, it won't happen again.'

'This is how much attention you pay in class? From tomorrow you won't sit there. You'll sit next to Zenab,' she said, pointing at the front row. 'Here onwards, I should not see anybody looking out of the window.'

Then she carried on: 'Wait. The reason why I was calling you was: you are not going for the picnic.'

'Why?'

'Because we cannot take responsibility for you. If you get hurt with your one leg, the whole school will be in trouble.'

Maryam moved her head with a jerk. 'I have two legs! See, here they are. Both my legs. One made of flesh and blood and the other of wood.'

This was her only opportunity to convince her class teacher. She had already felt the breeze looking out of the window from the bus, looking at the birds flying and humming her favourite songs. The last time she was on a bus was when her mother took her to her uncle's house. But she had not got the window seat then and people were standing standing all around her, falling on each other.

'Ma'am, wood is stronger. So, my parents got it replaced. I want to become a superhero. That's why. You'll see, one day I'll be able to fly because my left leg is lighter ...'

'Okay, okay, don't argue now. Bring your mother tomorrow. I'll explain it to her. You complicate everything.'

Maryam sat down, looking at the floor. Pigeon was still sitting there, looking at her. Maryam did not move for a long time. How would her mother meet Mandira Ma'am tomorrow? She had so much work to do that by the time she could come, it would be too late.

*If only I did not need help in getting ready for school, if only I could come to school by myself, Ammi would not have to get up so early to finish the household chores*, Maryam thought.

'You don't want to take me, it's fine.' Her voice broke as she said the words.

~

'Let's go out, Maryam. Let's have lunch.' Sara had been sitting next to Maryam waiting for the class to get over. She wanted to hold her tight. They had made so many plans together for the picnic.

'Why don't you call Aunty? She can explain how much you want to go for the picnic,' Sara suggested.

'How will Ammi come, Sara? She has to go to the haveli every day. She sits there all day on a cot with colourful threads all around her. She makes such beautiful flowers with them. Then she comes to pick me up. There are days she has to go back again. She hardly gets any rest. After we all go to sleep, she sits up till late with a dim candlelight to finish the pending embroidery orders. In either case, I would have got bored, Sara. It's good I'm not going.'

Sara knew it was not true.

When Zaheda came to pick her up from school that day, Maryam held her mother's hand as tight as she could. She tried to walk faster than usual. Maryam decided not to tell her mother about the picnic. Her mother tended to become sad and remorseful whenever Maryam brought up any topic related to her wooden leg. *I don't want her to feel bad*, Maryam thought.

When they reached home, Maryam asked, 'Ammi, can I help you?'

'Help me with what?'

'You tell me. Anything I can do. I want to be of some help.'

'Haha! You already help me so much by being my obedient child.'

So, Maryam sat in their bedroom, reading. There was only one bedroom in their house and one baithak (living room). When Maryam's father came back from work, Zaheda would put a durrie on the floor and sit there. Maryam was still sure she was not going to tell her mother about the picnic.

But she couldn't refrain from asking: 'Ammi, what is a picnic?'

'Picnic? Picnic is like a get-together where you go somewhere outdoors, have food together, play and have fun.'

That night, Maryam went to the terrace. 'Moon Angel, what do I do now? I cannot tell Ammi. She'll feel sad. But what am I going to tell her about why I won't go to school?'

Moon Angel said, 'You tell her everything. She'll be alright. She needs to know.'

'I'll not tell her anything. I'll just wander around after she drops me to school. I'll then come back to the school gate when it's time for her to pick me up.'

Moon Angel paused for a while. 'Do you know what happens to people who lie to their parents?'

'No. What happens?'

'Each time you lie, your wooden leg will keep getting longer and longer and then you won't be able to walk at all. If you continue to lie, you may even become a donkey.'

'Like a real donkey?'

'Yes, a real donkey.'

As Maryam slowly climbed down the stairs, she tried to imagine what it would be like to walk with a longer leg.

～

The next day, as Maryam was coming out of the school gate, she suddenly remembered what Moon Angel had said. '*Let me give it a try*' she thought. Maryam went to the ice cream seller. 'One chocolate ice cream!'

'Stick or cone?'

'The ten-rupees one.'

Maryam took the icecream in her hand and started to walk away. The icecream seller stopped her and asked for the money. 'I already gave it to you,' Maryam said.

'Oh … I must have kept it inside then,' the icecream seller said as he started searching for it in his small bag. He had seen Maryam before. He had noticed how she, unlike other children, would come with her mother every day, holding her hand. He would feel sorry for her. *Why would she lie? Maybe she gave it to me and I forgot,* he thought. He nodded and said, 'Okay.' Maryam started walking towards Haji Chacha's shop.

But she could not forget the face of the icecream seller when he nodded and said 'okay' to her. Her leg felt heavier than ever as she walked. She wanted to go back and tell him the truth. But she kept walking. She was staggering more than usual today. She did not even stop to smell the samosas at Bade Miyan's shop. He had just taken them out.

As she crossed his shop looking down, Bade Miyan called out to her, 'Maryam, is everything alright at home? Where is your mother?'

Maryam did not look up. 'Ammi had a few deliveries to make today. So, she asked me to wait at Haji Chacha's shop.' Haji Chacha's shop was only a stone's throw away from school. But today it seemed farther than anywhere she had ever been on foot. By the time Maryam reached Haji Chacha's shop, it had started drizzling.

*All of this had to happen today*, she thought, even though she usually liked looking at the sky when it rained.

'Did my wooden leg grow longer?' Maryam wondered. 'Will it ever get back to its normal size?'

When Zaheda arrived, Maryam could not wait to hug her.

'Is everything alright?' Zaheda asked.

'Ammi, I am a bad girl. I lied to the icecream bhaiya and did not pay for the icecream. That's why my leg has grown bigger and I cannot walk properly. If I lie like this, I'll become a donkey.'

Zaheda would have ordinarily scolded her for this. She was very particular about the values her children developed. Once she was about to slap Maryam for lying about picking up a needle. Shamima at the haveli managed to stop her.

'What are you doing? She has lied. Will she stop lying if you beat her?'

'You don't understand, Shamima. The only legacy I can give to my children is values. The house we stay in is the ancestral property of Maryam's father. They'll get that from him. What will I give to my daughters? Just this. Values. All that I earn gets spent on household expenses. I don't know when it goes before the month ends. School fees, books, food, electricity, gas ... it's all so expensive these days. You know how Maryam's father has work sometimes while at other times he has to go around all day in the sun looking for work. He comes home so exhausted. I have to ensure that our children are raised properly. That they have the same values that we got from our parents and grandparents. Who else will do that? You tell me.'

'I understand, Zaheda. Getting daughters married these days is not easy. You need a lot of money,' Shamima said.

'I'm more worried about Maryam's education. There's no one at home to guide her. She has to be self-reliant. See, Saima, my elder daughter can manage. She can study from anywhere till we find someone for her. She can continue her studies or work, depending on the kind of house she gets. It all depends on luck, you see. So, we just have to save for her wedding. But Maryam's situation is different. She will have to earn for herself. I want the best for both my daughters. I do not want Maryam to beg for help.'

'Oh yes, she'll need help. You won't be there for her all her life,' Shamima said.

'That's my worry, Shamima,' Zaheda said with tears in her eyes.

'I have heard people in America do not have to worry about such things. But then America is America.' Zaheda sighed.

～

'Ammi, Ammi, are you upset with me?' This time, Zaheda did not scold her.

'Come, let's go home first. We can talk later.'

But Maryam insisted that she did not want to go home. She wanted to go to the haveli.

'But why?'

'Just like that. You need not drop me home first. I can sit and wait at the haveli till you finish your work. We'll go home together.'

Zaheda and Maryam started walking. 'But what about my leg?' Maryam asked. 'It still feels heavy.'

'Now that you have told me the truth, it will be fine. I'll give the money for the icecream to Bhaiya tomorrow.'

When Maryam reached the haveli holding Zaheda's hand, she found the usual scene before her. All the women sitting in their corners, against the pillars or on a cot doing their work holding a piece of cloth and a needle.

'Amma, how's your lover?'

'Huh, at this age a widow like me will have a lover?'

'Why not!'

All the women started laughing. Amma would get annoyed easily, but she enjoyed these conversations. Amma had become a widow at a very young age. She had stayed indoors most of the time, first at her in-laws' place and then in her maternal home. After her brother's death, she'd turned her maternal home into an abode for these women during the day. Amma finally got to enjoy the world through their eyes.

'The sharbat is really nice today. What did you add ... Oh, look who's here.'

'Maryam, come beta. Why are you standing there? Come to Amma.'

'Will you have some fruits, Maryam?' Falguni asks.

'Why would she have old people's food? Give her some sharbat and get some pakoras and samosas from Bade Miyan's shop. And don't forget the chutney!'

'What did you do in school today? Sit comfortably. Wait, let me get you a stool.'

'Here it is. Now tell me, what did you do in school today?'

'As if you know what happens in school, Amma.' Everyone started laughing.

'Shut up! My daughter went to school till Class 8.'

Soon, the hot, crispy pakoras and samosas arrived. With chutney—both green and orange. Maryam was particularly fond of the green chutney into which Bade Miyan would put extra tamarind for her. At least that's what he said he did.

'Come, come. Everyone, come.'

The women pulled up chairs and stools for themselves, sat around the cot, and started eating from the plate.

'This chutney is so good. It's the best I ever had,' Shamima said.

Maryam smiled.

As the women kept giggling and laughing, Nikhat brought out a ludo board.

'Come, Maryam. Let's play!'

'And who'll do your work, Nikhat? Amma?'

There was laughter.

'Why do you all drag Amma into everything!' Amma exclaimed as she got up to wash her hands.

Maryam liked it here at the haveli. Nobody stared at her wooden leg or pretended about anything. It was all so normal.

*Is this what a picnic is like?* Maryam wondered. *Where everyone goes somewhere outdoors, has food together, plays and has fun together. Isn't that what Amma said? Wow, this is a picnic!*

∽

Before going up to the terrace that night, Maryam had no idea that the conversation she was going to have with Moon Angel would shape her life for years to come.

'Maryam, I'm very happy about what you did today. You told the truth to your mother. I am giving you a boon. From here on, you'll have a life where you get to make your own choices. You choose a bad option, you have to pay back. You choose a good one, you get a reward. It may take a while for the rewards to reach you, but they will definitely come.'

'But these things will keep happening again and again. It always happens to me. Mandira Ma'am told me in front of the whole class that I cannot go for the picnic. Nobody thought about how it would make me feel. Even Mandira Ma'am didn't.'

'Maryam, are you feeling bad because you are feeling inferior to your classmates? Is it about the picnic at all?' Moon Angel asked.

Maryam was quiet. She closed her eyes.

'I felt as if I was being discarded. Yes, I do feel inferior to my classmates because I was told I couldn't do what they could. But I could have gone for the picnic. Then why did Mandira Ma'am say I cannot go?'

'You cannot be a puppet, Maryam. People will do things, say things.'

'I can choose?' Maryam was confused.

'Yes, you can choose how you want to feel no matter what people say.'

'Maryam, whatever happens, just remember you are my worthy child and nobody can take that away from you unless you yourself choose it that way.' Moon Angel said.

In the end, Maryam did not go for the picnic. Sara did not go either. Instead, she came to Maryam's house. They played with dolls all morning. Maryam took Sara with her to the haveli in the afternoon. They played there all day. Amma was happy to have a new visitor. She bought pakoras and samosas from Bade Miyan's shop. And yes, with the green chutney!

# The Swan in Disguise

## *by O Aishwarya*

ZARA LAY IN BED, READING HER BRAILLE BOOK UNDER the covers, knowing that the light outside was slowly getting brighter and brighter. She was reluctant to get up because she knew today was going to be just horrible.

She rolled over, picked up her phone and checked the time. '7:01 a.m.,' said the mechanical, vaguely robotic-sounding voice of her screen reader. Her school bus would arrive at 8.00 a.m. She didn't care. She didn't want to go to school. But Mummy would be here any moment to wake her up.

Knock knock. 'Zara,' her mother called. 'You'll miss the bus again if you don't wake up this instant.'

Quick as a flash, Zara hid the book under the covers, curled up around it, and pretended to be asleep. She knew what was coming next. And sure enough, just as she'd thought, her mother opened the door and peeped in.

'Zara!' her mother called again.

'Hmm … I feel sick today.'

'Nonsense. Don't forget I've known you ever since you were born.'

'Really, Mummy. My tummy hurts.'

'Is that the same tummy ache you have every school day?' Zara could hear the laughter in her mother's words.

'But Mummy …'

'That's enough now,' said Mummy, in a tone that brooked no argument. 'Get up this instant if you don't want me to douse you in cold water. I don't understand why you always make such a big fuss about going to school. And today's the first day of this year, too. Aren't you excited at all?'

'No,' groaned Zara, rubbing her eyes and slowly sitting up. 'I hate school.'

Zara knew this troubled her parents. She had overheard Mummy talking on the phone to Ashwathi Aunty about it the other day.

'I just don't understand why Zara makes such a big fuss about going to school,' Mummy had said. 'It's not like she hates studying, either. She loves reading and writing, and gets good grades. I don't understand what the problem is.'

~

The truth was that Zara had a secret, and her greatest fear was that somebody, especially her parents, would find out about it. And there would be a big row. So Zara muddled along with her secret as best she could.

You see, Zara was friendless. The other children at school bullied her, made fun of her, and never let her join in their games or secrets or talks. What would Mummy and Daddy say if they knew? They would definitely be unhappy. Mummy would, perhaps, even cry. Mummy was always sad when something happened to highlight that Zara wasn't quite like the other children. Besides, thinking and imagining that Zara had friends made Mummy happy.

And her daddy? He always said, 'It is better to just ignore mean people because they are only trying to get a rise out of you.' Somehow, trying to explain her school life to her parents always felt like explaining to a whale what it was like to live in a forest.

It made her blood boil to think of them now, her beastly classmates. Always taunting and making hurtful remarks, just because she was a bit different from them. Freak, ghost-eyes, ugly duckling.

'Some people need a sign to tell them they don't belong,' one would start.

'Why can't you just go and study in one of those schools ... you know ... those special schools?'

It had always been like this. Ever since Zara could remember. *What would it be like to relax in school?* she wondered. To not have to worry every second of every minute?

~

The first day of a new year was always exciting. There were new classrooms to be looked at and appraised in comparison to the previous ones, new cupboards and cubby holes to fill, and most important of all, new classmates to meet.

Zara had no hopes of befriending any of them. She had tried in the past and been disappointed too many times for her to even think of it now. Most of the new children were extremely awkward around blind people, and didn't know what to say or do. Anyway, within a few days, they quickly realized the pecking order of the class.

But this time, this time was different.

When Zara walked into the class, trying to judge which benches had free seats from the sounds of her classmates, a friendly voice hailed her.

'Hi!' It was a girl, a girl who sounded upbeat and chirpy.

'Hello.'

'I'm new here. Do you mind if I ... uh ... sit with you?' The same girl, voice a little uncertain now.

'Sure.' Zara shrugged indifferently. Why did it matter who sat next to her? This new girl would follow the lead of the others soon enough.

'I'm Niranjana,' she said. 'And you are?'

'Zara.'

Over the course of the day, Zara found out that Niranjana's mother was a schoolteacher who had been appointed this year, and that Niranjana and her family had just moved here from another state.

Zara marvelled at Niranjana's comfort with blindness. She didn't talk down to her in condescending tones, offer help unnecessarily, or ask intrusive questions about how Zara became blind. She wasn't unduly surprised at Zara writing in Braille or walking with a cane, either. Nothing seemed to faze her.

～

Towards the end of the day, their teacher announced something interesting, something that had the whole class in an uproar.

'This month,' she said, 'we're going to be conducting our class assembly.'

'What's that?' Niranjana asked Zara, leaning closer to hear, but the teacher wasn't done yet.

'As some of you might know,' she continued, 'every week, a class is chosen to conduct the big assembly in front of the whole school. This includes many important jobs, such as saying prayers for others to repeat, reading aloud the important news of the day, and presenting a short entertainment programme for everyone to enjoy. The entertainment programme could involve anything creative, such as dances, songs, plays, or anything else you might be able to think of.'

It took ages for the ruckus to die down; everyone seemed to have a lot of ideas for what they should do.

'Let's have a dance performance,' said Reshma, who was a graceful dancer.

'That wouldn't be fair to all your classmates,' said their teacher. 'Not everyone can dance as well as you.'

'A musical show!' said George.

'Same problem,' said the teacher. 'We need to do something that everybody can have a role in. Something in which everybody's talents can be showcased.'

As the class discussed the programme, Niranjana turned to Zara again.

'Aren't you excited?' she asked in a low whisper.

'Why? Why should I be?' she answered, shrugging. 'They'll give me some uninteresting task to do just because I'm blind.'

She sounded bitter and self-pitying, even to her own ears.

'But why? Being blind doesn't limit you from taking part in the class assembly,' Niranjana replied, sounding genuinely surprised.

Zara was spared from having to answer by the teacher ordering the class to quiet down.

'A play would perhaps be the best idea,' she said. 'Things such as little bits of music and small dances can be added to it. What do you say?'

The class cheered.

'What kind of play should it be?'

'I know. What about a fairy tale? We could even do some of the songs and dances that way,' suggested Reneetta, a quiet girl whom Zara barely knew.

'That sounds like a good idea. Does everyone agree?'

Everyone did.

Despite herself, Zara felt her spirits rising. She loved fairy tales. Perhaps this assembly might be fun after all.

~

The next morning, Zara got to school a little early. There was still around half an hour for the bell to go. As she walked into the class, she idly noted the babble of voices, all from the right half of the room.

'... can't do that, Stephy,' Reshma was saying.

'Yeah.' That voice was Angela's. 'I mean ... just think of all the props we'll have to make for the Little Mermaid to look realistic.'

'Hmm. You're right,' said Stephy. 'Let's see.'

The sound of someone flipping the pages of a book followed. Maybe they were looking at a book of fairy tales.

'Hey, how about Little Red Riding Hood?'

'Yeah. It's all about obedience and things like that, right? The teachers will love it.' That was Annie.

Zara had no intention of crossing paths with Annie and her gang first thing in the morning, so she headed over to her bench to put her things down.

'You're taking part in the auditions today, right?'

It was Niranjana, the new girl who'd sat with her the day before.

'Me?' Zara asked, incredulously.

'Yes. Which role do you fancy?' Niranjana was undaunted.

'What's this?' Zara knew that voice. How could she not, featuring as it did in her worst nightmares? That was Annie's voice. Annie, the golden girl whom everyone liked, including the teachers. Annie, who looked down on anyone who was different and didn't fit in. 'Why, Zara, I didn't know you had a talent for acting,' she went on in a sickly sweet voice. 'Fancy one of the lead roles, do you?'

'Her?' And there was her beloved sidekick Angela, as unangelic as it was possible to be. Ugh! She knew what was coming next. She had tried so hard to avoid this.

'What's your problem?' asked Niranjana, turning around to face them. 'We weren't talking to you.'

'Oh, nothing. We just found it funny. The fact that Zara wants to act.'

'Why?' Niranjana again, faint puzzlement in her voice.

'She's blind!' said Annie, like it was a big pronouncement.

'Congratulations for stating the obvious,' said Niranjana, her voice steeped in sarcasm. 'Of course a newcomer shouldn't be expected to understand that from the cane, the Brailler, and the Braille textbooks. But what's your point?'

'Er ... what?' said Annie.

'What does her being blind have to do with the play and its auditions?'

'Blind people can't act!'

'Why not? Is there a law against that?'

'Er ...'

'Well, my mother is blind too. I've seen and known blind people all my life, enough to know that it is not your responsibility to decide what Zara should do. So buzz off.'

Zara was shocked. No wonder Niranjana was unfazed by her blindness. No wonder she didn't ask unnecessary questions about her Brailler that she could have just googled anyway. Niranjana's mother was blind.

Zara had never met another blind person in her life.

'What role would she be fit for anyway?' Annie asked rhetorically, not having a cutting comeback ready in time.

'I know, the ugly duckling,' said Angela.

Everyone except Zara and Niranjana began to laugh.

'Oh, you're so disgusting,' Niranjana fired back. 'Come on, Zara. Let's go.'

As they marched out together, Zara could hear the low whispers.

'Yeah …'

'Saw her yesterday …'

'Teaches the ninth and tenth graders …'

'Math …'

'Stephy says she really knows her stuff …'

'And she's blind …'

'Can't believe it …'

Niranjana's mother was blind. She hadn't got over that fact yet. But, at long last, Zara was not alone after a bullying incident. At last, she had a friend with her.

~

They walked on quietly for a while. Zara's head was whirling. Was she, really, the Ugly Duckling? Was that how others thought of her? A misfit, someone they hoped would go away? She was unwanted, too, and made fun of wherever she went. Nobody liked her. And she herself felt like she didn't belong, would never belong among these ducks who didn't understand her.

She didn't even have a friend.

But that wasn't entirely true, she thought to herself. Niranjana had defended her, spoken up for her. But why had she? Zara wondered. Was it sympathy? Pity for the girl who was being bullied?

'Why?' Zara asked abruptly. 'Why did you stand up for me?'

'Well … Why wouldn't I? She's a bully. Also, I just don't see her point. You're blind. But why on earth should that mean you shouldn't act in the play?'

'Have you seen a lot of blind people like me?'

'Well … whether they're like you or not I don't know, but yes. I have seen many people who are blind. Some are my mother's friends, and some my elder sister's.'

'Is she blind too? Your elder sister?'

'Yes.'

What was it like, Zara wondered, to have lots of people around who were going through the same issues as you were. She wished she could talk to somebody, anybody, who was blind.

'But I don't understand those kids in there. Why should they think blindness will get in the way?' Niranjana was apparently still puzzled.

'Errr …' Zara was at a loss as to what to say. But then she realized with a vague sense of puzzlement that she was angry. The whirling, churning feeling in her gut was coalescing into a razor-like rage that she was hard-pressed to control.

'What do you even know about it, anyway? You have no idea what it's like … how they treat me.'

'I just saw that, remember?'

Niranjana's voice was still calm, and, irrationally, Zara grew even more angry at hearing it.

'No! Just because you've been here for a day does not mean you know everything. Do you even have any idea what it's like to always be sidelined? I'm actually dreading the class assembly now. You want to know why, do you? It's because I'll definitely be stuck reciting the prayer or reading the news or something equally unimportant and boring. I have never danced on the stage, or acted, or even taken part in a tableau. Do you know that? Don't assume you know how I feel.'

Zara realized she was on the verge of shouting. How had this conversation gone so wrong?

'Stop taking out your anger on me. I'm not the one who's bullying you. And in case you haven't noticed, I'm trying to stop them.'

Now Niranjana sounded angry, too. Good.

'But why? I still don't understand why you want to be friends with me.' And then, hesitantly, Zara voiced her hidden, secret fear. 'Is it because you feel sorry for me? You know ... Because of the blindness and the bullying?'

'Of course not!' Niranjana sounded amazed.

'Why did you sit with me yesterday?'

'Honestly? Because I saw that nobody else did. My sister was isolated in school, too. A bit. And I wondered if you were like that, too.'

'I'm not ... I'm not something like your charity case.'

Zara felt tears spring into her eyes. She pulled her hand out of Niranjana's, and turned away, almost running towards the class.

'Wait! Zara, wait! I didn't mean it like that.'

But Zara was in no mood to listen. She had had enough.

～

Back at home, Zara couldn't concentrate on her homework or her library book. Her mind was abuzz with thoughts. The Ugly Duckling. The *Ugly* Duckling. The phrase kept repeating in her mind, over and over again like one of those old cassettes stuck in the music player. She was unwanted at school, she knew that, but was she, perhaps, unwanted at home, too? Was she a burden to her parents? Even Niranjana only felt pity for her, not true friendship. Maybe she shouldn't stay here, a nuisance to everybody.

Could she run away? But where could she go? What could she do?

Nobody wanted her.

She was the Ugly Duckling.

The thought ignited a fiery mix of anger and hatred inside her. Hatred against a world that did not let her, and others like her, live in peace. Anger at the world who thought a blind person was someone lower than them. With hardly a thought, she sped out the door, not knowing where she was going, or why, but something inside her couldn't help it. All she could think about was how much she wanted to get away from everybody. She would go to the park for a while. She needed some space to think.

～

Zara didn't know how long she sat on the swing, letting it take her higher and higher as she brooded over the injustice of it all. It could have been an hour. Or a minute. She had no idea. She simply sat there, letting the wind cool her hot face and wet cheeks.

She needed some space and time to think, to simmer down, and she took it, ignoring the constantly vibrating phone in her pocket.

Would it always be like this? she asked herself. Wasn't there a way out of this entire mess? And she had snapped at the only person who had wanted to make friends with her.

'Do you know what time it is, Zara?' the voice startled her and she jumped.

'Who are you?' The voice belonged to a stranger. How did he know who she was? Thoughts about kidnappers and child abusers ran through her mind, and with them came the cautionary words of her parents on the dangers of talking to strangers.

'I'm from the police. Your parents called us to report that you were missing.'

They must have been frantic, she thought. And she hadn't answered her phone. But she had just wanted to be alone.

As the police officer spoke to her parents on the phone, assuring them that she was safe and unharmed, she got up, wondering what on earth she would tell her parents. She was in for it now, she was sure of it.

~

There was a profound silence.

Zara's hands were wrapped around the mug full of hot chocolate as she sat there, head bowed.

'Zara.' No answer. 'Zara.' She didn't even look up.

'Zara, please. Please tell us why you did this.' It was her father's voice, heavy with disappointment.

'You have to talk to us, Zara dear,' Mummy said, her hand slung around Zara's shoulders. 'If you don't open up to us, how can we do something about it? How can we help you?'

'You can't help me. Nobody can.'

'Why don't you try us?'

Zara stood up, her voice rising uncontrollably. 'Well, maybe, because I've tried before? You can't help me. You only know how to cry, Mummy. And, Daddy, you can only give me stupid advice about how I should just ignore the bullies. You know what? Ignoring them doesn't help.'

'Zara, sit down,' said Daddy in his stern no-arguments tone. 'Do you mean that you're being bullied at school? How long has this been going on?'

'From when I started going to school. It's always been like this. Forever.'

'Dear God!' Mummy's voice was close to breaking already. 'Why did God choose my daughter for this too? Hasn't she suffered enough already?'

Her voice broke off into sobs.

'See? I told you! All you can do is cry. Or even worse, tell me it's my fate or something. Isn't that what you've been doing every time I bring a problem to you?'

'Zara, that's enough,' said her father. 'Use a respectful tone while talking to your mother, please.'

Zara shook her head wearily. Running away was a bad idea. All it had managed to do was bring her secret to her parents' attention. And look where that had got her.

'I don't want to discuss this,' said Zara. 'You don't understand, anyway. Neither of you do.'

'Wait, Zara,' said her father. 'This conversation is not over. Why didn't you tell us?'

'You only cry or give sage advice that does not really help,' Zara replied. 'Just like you're doing now,' she added pointedly.

'And you felt bad about upsetting us, right?' Daddy asked shrewdly.

'Well, yes …'

'Zara, dear, we'll figure out a way to fix this. First, let's call your principal, and then maybe your class teacher, to see what can be done. Don't worry. We can fix this bullying problem.'

Zara just shrugged. It was always better not to hope. That way, there would be no disappointment later.

~

Things happened very quickly after that. The calls to the principal and the teachers, the appointment with the school counsellor, and best of all, the talks with Niranjana's Mummy, who was also a teacher in the school, and somewhat of an expert on blindness too, being blind herself.

Zara's stunt had scared her parents and showed them how serious the problem was. It had scared Zara, too. She never wanted to feel that way again, as though her insides were boiling and churning with emotions that had not been let out for a long, long time. Talking about it helped, especially when the person she was talking to was Niranjana's Mummy.

She helped her to understand her blindness, and to sort out how she thought about it.

'Is it a bad thing to be blind?' Zara remembered asking one day.

'No, Zara, not at all,' said Niranjana's mother. 'I know many people have made you feel that way. Like the kids in school, when they bullied you and made fun of you because you are blind. But tell me truthfully, why do you think it is so bad to be blind? Is it really being blind that causes problems for you, or is it how people treat you because of it?'

'How people treat me, I guess,' Zara replied. 'I mean, I know I can do most things my classmates can, but they always automatically think I can't. And that bothers me.'

'We'll just have to show them, Zara. They haven't been exposed to many disabled people, you know. You are the first disabled person most of them have interacted with, so they treat you differently. But they will change, too, once they have more exposure.'

'They even said they think I can act only as the Ugly Duckling. In the play for the class assembly, I mean,' Zara said miserably.

'Well ... haven't you understood the point of the story, Zara? The Ugly Duckling thought she was ugly and a misfit, but then she realized that she was just different. All the time, until she met the swans, she was looking at her appearance through the eyes of the ducks. He thought she was ugly because the ducks thought she was.'

'I never thought of it that way!' she exclaimed. 'I haven't seen any blind people, either. Till now that is.'

'We'll see about that.' Aunty sounded thoughtful.

∼

'Listen,' Niranjana said a couple of days after their fight. 'Can I talk to you?'

'Alright,' said Zara, reluctantly.

'I'm sorry,' said Niranjana. 'About what I said the other day. I didn't mean it that way, you know ... I'm not friends with you only because you're blind or because I pity you. Well, initially I did sit with you because I thought all the others were isolating you. But it wasn't pity or anything. I do genuinely like you. You have an amazing sense of humour, and you've read more books than the rest of our classmates put together.'

Zara smiled. 'It's okay. I shouldn't have yelled at you either. I was just really angry.'

And from that moment on, they were firm friends.

'I heard you are going to the convention this year,' said Niranjana.

Zara nodded. 'Yes. Your mom told Mummy that it will be good for me.'

'You are so lucky,' said Niranjana enviously. 'I've been to this event a couple of times, and it's amazing.'

'Really?'

'Yes. You'll see.'

~

Zara thoroughly enjoyed her experience at the convention. Until the day she and her family arrived at the hotel where the convention was taking place, she had only seen one blind person in her entire life—Niranjana's mother.

Zara met many many new people, made many friends, both blind and sighted, who were of her age, and met new mentors and role models who showed her that nothing was impossible just because she was blind. She was slowly beginning to understand what Niranjana's mother had been talking about. Some of the children there had also gone through similar experiences with bullying, and could talk to her about what they did to combat it.

But what she enjoyed the most was that, wherever she went, she was not the only blind person in the room. At the convention she was just another kid, and she loved it.

Adults had serious discussions about God only knew what; meanwhile children were running around everywhere, chatting, playing, and making new friends; and underlying it all, was the rhythmic tapping and clicking of a thousand long white canes.

She came back from the convention reenergized. Zara wasn't completely alright, but she felt less alone now. Slowly, she was beginning to build up a support system to turn to for help when she needed it.

～

'Ready, Zara?' her teacher asked, as they waited behind the stage for her turn to come.

Right on cue, a voice proclaimed, 'Next up is a play titled "Swan in Disguise", a retelling of the fairy tale The Ugly Duckling. The script for the story was written by Zara, who is also playing the role of the mother duck.'

As Zara and her classmates took to the stage in the wake of the school's applause, she couldn't help but think back to the moment when, in an effort to taunt her again, Annie had suggested The Ugly Duckling as a possible play they could perform.

'Why not ... I think that could work,' their teacher had said, unaware of Annie's real intentions.

'I don't really like the ending, though.' For the first time, Zara voiced her opinion about something the class was doing. 'I mean, why can't the swan stay with the duck family? They were her family after all. She shouldn't have to fly away and live with the swans just because she discovered she was one of them.'

'Why don't you rewrite it, then?' the teacher suggested. 'Make your own version of it. And maybe we could all perform that.'

'We can rewrite the story?' Zara had asked, surprised. 'I mean, we're allowed to do that? It's a fairy tale after all.'

'Of course we can,' their teacher had replied. 'In fact, the stories we now know as fairy tales were once passed down orally through generations. Don't you think they might have changed the stories up a bit to suit their particular audience? In fact, even famous compilers of fairy tales, like the Brothers Grimm, did change up some things. People have been rewriting fairy tales for centuries now, and famous fairy tales like Cinderella and The Little Mermaid have hundreds of versions, all written by people of different cultures and regions.'

'Wow!' The class was amazed.

And that was how Zara had come to write the script for the play.

As the children in Zara's class worked with her on the play, there was slowly a reduction in the bullying and hostility she had to face. This process was also helped by Niranjana and her mother, who enabled the children to celebrate each other's differences by subtly educating them through interesting movies, books, videos and life histories. The children also realized that the post-convention Zara was a person to be reckoned with, who didn't hesitate to give back as good as she got. Zara was slowly coming to celebrate her own body, and thus was harder to bully.

'I don't know why,' said Reshma one day as they all worked together on the play, 'I am not so curious about your blindness anymore. It's just there, you know? Just another part of you.'

'That's the point I've been trying to make for years,' Zara said.

Zara would perhaps never be able to be friends with Annie, Angela or a few others in the class. She wasn't a saint after all. But a stalemate was soon arrived at.

As Zara played her role on stage, Niranjana, in her role as the swan, proclaimed, 'I wasn't an ugly duckling after all! I was just a swan in disguise!' And Zara vowed to continue the work she had begun. It was by no means easy, and she knew she wasn't yet at a stage where she could completely celebrate her differences and feel pride in her disability, but she would get there one day, she promised herself. She was a swan among duck, after all, and was finally beginning to find her place in both communities.

Just as Zara had written out a happily ever after for the swan in the play, she would, she thought determinedly, craft out a happily ever after for herself.

# Red

## *by Sarani*

WICKED IS THE COLOUR RED.

Biddy lay on the floor curled up like an infant, clutching her knees tightly with both her hands, her chin resting on them. She was filled with disgust and horror, a deep guilt rising in her throat. What if she did? What if she didn't? Would she have stopped at the right moment? Would she have wanted to? Questions swirled around in her mind, spinning out of control. Paralysed by her thoughts, Biddy lay curled up, bathed in the sunlight.

~

The year Biddy was born, her mother's world was plagued with war. The village folk still call it the time of the Big Bad Wolf. There were snarling wolf-skin demons plundering village after village, murdering and raping innocents. No living being could escape them; no number of prayers to any god could halt their march into battle. So many villagers took refuge in the Dark Woods.

Biddy's mother trudged far to hide under the thick canopy of the Dark Woods. It was a misty dark night, and the leaves of the trees were bellowing in fury. She lay on the forest floor, damp and cold, while above her the sky was the colour of blood with patches of jet black. The smell of burning flesh crept up her nose and eerie black smoke rose behind her. The shrieking screams of villagers rang in her ears. She laid a gentle hand on her swollen belly; she could feel her child move inside her. Pain was scorching through her body. She clutched her crimson velvet hooded robe for support. The baby was coming soon. She felt a tingling on the back of her neck, a premonition that something sinister was about to happen. She closed her eyes and opened them slowly and valiantly started to search the deep void of darkness. She heard a cracking and then a sudden deafening sound engulf the deep silence. She could see her village clearly in the distance; angry fires were dancing like silhouettes of belly dancers swaying their hips. She heard the echo of the invading army, singing merrily in union. Pain shot through her body, as she clenched her teeth in agony.

~

By the time the sun tiptoed shyly through the grey clouds in the crimson sky, Biddy's mother was able to walk slowly and unsteadily towards the roaring flames of her village, a bundle wrapped in her red hooded robe. The baby quietly gazed at her mother's face, unaware of the sounds unfolding.

Years passed. Biddy and her mother lived in a lodging built of stone at the edge of the woods. Remnants of war still surrounded the village borders, in a graveyard of fireflies. Soon after Biddy's birth, the king of the land sought assistance from a mercenary army from a far-off land. Months of battle passed until the earth was soaked with blood and the river ran red, while corpses of the nemeses lay side by side: brothers in death. The army defeated the wolf people, and any that remained sought refuge in the mountain peaks beyond the Dark Woods. As more time passed, the wolf people simply became dark bedtime stories.

Biddy grew up a cheerful and joyful child. She spent her day picking wildflowers from the fields and meadows, making them into wreaths and crowns. She may have been this way for she was unaware of the evil and darkness around her. When she came to this world, she was incapable of hearing. Her world was one of quiet silence, a world where no sound could be heard. The day her life began, surrounded by the sounds of death and destruction of the village, she only heard silence. She did not miss the boundless sounds of the earth, for she did not know what they sounded like. She did not hear the shrieking sound of the peacock, but only saw its beautiful vibrant colours as it danced. She did not hear the sound of a shotgun, but saw the village huntsman point it towards an elk, who would lie down to sleep. The dissolution of her surroundings never tainted her, therefore her smile was like a rainbow that never faded from the sky.

~

Often Biddy would go to visit her grandmother, keeping safely to the path at the edge of the Dark Woods. She took with her the crowns and garlands she made out of wildflowers, and a basket full of treats her mother baked. Biddy loved visiting the old lady, and she loved the tales her grandmother would tell her: of time gone past, of kingdoms far far away, of handsome princes and enchanting princesses, of gallant brave knights and a pond of water wider than fields and meadows, of the floating wooden house as large as a mountain drifting on this pond. Even though she couldn't hear grandmother's voice, she understood the silent words, and her grandmother understood Biddy's replies. Her grandmother would make sure she moved her mouth distinctly with each syllable so Biddy could lip-read—when Biddy was little, her grandmother had taught her how to do this. The villagers also always talked slowly to make sure she understood, but some of the village men covered their mouths when speaking, and Biddy did not find it easy to understand what they were saying. But Biddy enjoyed her grandmother's stories, and dreamed of visiting these faraway lands herself one day. Her grandmother always ended each tale by telling Biddy, 'Dear, you must never talk to strange men.'

So it happened that one early morning, Biddy was carrying a basket of treats and a fresh loaf of bread. She carried in her left hand a crown of wildflowers she had made earlier that morning. She was wearing her mother's red velvet hooded robe, its edges embroidered with white calla lilies. Her mother had given it to her a fortnight ago as a gift to celebrate her becoming a young woman. Biddy's mother put the robe on her, raised the hood over her head and pressed her lips gently on her daughter's forehead. But as she did this, she sighed a dejected sigh. She told her daughter as she always did, to never enter the Dark Woods and never stray from the path. That was the rule of the little village where they lived; the village folks would frown upon anybody who defied this mantra.

Biddy slowly walked down the familiar path at the edge of the Dark Woods, and as she neared her grandmother's house, she saw in the distance, leaning idly against a tree, a strange man. As she drew closer, he gPritied her and smiled. She noticed the man was wearing a thick grey fur coat, white tunic and black leather trousers. The man smiled at her, his silver canines sparkling brilliantly. He had a diamond-shaped face with hollow cheekbones, and his eyes were yellow and narrow, with irises as black as coal. His ears were pointy and close to the side of his neck, and his hair was the colour of wheat fields and hung in ringlets around his gaunt face.

Biddy felt uneasy, especially when his smile turned to annoyance when she could not understand what he was saying. All she could make out was the word 'deaf', so she asked: 'What is deaf? Can you please talk slowly—I do not understand your words.'

That is what her grandmother had taught her to say, if she found it hard to understand someone. His face changed, he smiled cheekily, and gPritied her again, this time with a little sweetness in his words. 'Hello, pretty girl.' He smiled. Biddy's cheeks turned crimson as he drew closer to her, asking, 'What's your name?'

Biddy timidly said to him, 'I am not supposed to speak to strangers.'

He tilted his head and smiled, but his eyes showed irritation. Facing her directly and talking slower, he said, 'And who may I ask told you that?'

She nervously told him, 'My grandmother.' Her face was turning redder.

He narrowed his eyes and, smiling ominously, said, 'But aren't all friends strangers before you meet them?' Biddy thought for a moment. She knew only the folks who lived in her little village, and lived among them her whole life, so she could not make up her mind. But she nodded in acceptance.

He asked her where her grandmother lived and she gestured towards where the cottage stood. 'It's just beyond the cherry trees up ahead, can you see them?' she asked, looking down at her feet to cover her shy smile. 'I am on my way to deliver this basket of goodies and bread.' She lifted the basket. 'And this crown I made her this morning from the flowers I picked in the meadow.' She held the crown up to show him, looking at him through her lashes.

They spent hours talking. He asked her where she lived, who lived with her, and all about the little village. She answered his questions openly without hesitation. She told him about the wildflowers growing in the meadows, and how she loved making crowns and wreaths. And she told him the tales her grandmother would tell when she visited her. The sun was gleaming brilliantly high in the pale blue sky when she realized that she was on her way to her grandmother's house. She excused herself, but before she could leave he knelt beside her, lowered his face and spoke slowly. His forehead had formed crinkles, and smiling wickedly, he told her to meet him tomorrow, just before the sky turned red. He promised to take her deep into the woods, where flowers more beautiful than the flowers in her crown grew, so she could make crowns with them.

Then in a whisper, he told her, with his pointy finger and a sharp claw-like nail against his lips, to keep it a secret. She asked him why she needed to keep it a secret, and he said, 'Don't you whisper secrets with your friend?'

Biddy never understood if she ever had friends, so she nodded in agreement. He stood up and blew her a parting kiss and then started walking toward the Dark Woods. Watching him walk away made Biddy's stomach churn. She had a deep yearning in her heart for him, and was sad to see him go. She yearned for their next meeting, for him to be with her, talking, and for the time to stand still in this moment. She bit her lip and ran towards him. She managed to catch up just as he was about to step into the woods. She placed a hand on his shoulder to get his attention. He turned slowly looking down at her, a wide grin of satisfaction on his face. Their bodies were tightly pressed against each other. He put his hand around her, holding her close.

Biddy felt frightened and yet she felt her heart flutter at his touch; she could feel the wild rhythm of her heart, when the wolf asked, 'Why is your heart beating so fast?'

Embarrassed, she took a deep breath and said, 'Would you like to come with me to see my grandmother? She would love to meet you.'

The wolf stopped grinning. Biddy felt as though she had offended him, so she bowed her head in shame. She felt something sharp on her chin that forced her to look up. She saw his thick lips move, realizing it was his finger that felt sharp. Their faces were very close, and he was smiling again at her, with shifty eyes. He said, 'I will visit her later together with you.' He smiled and started to sing, merrily swaying her gently in his arms. Biddy looked at his mouth wide-eyed, gazing at his glossy pink lips moving as the syllables formed into words—

*Come little children into the dark … Tra la la la la …*

When he finished, he placed his lips against hers and kissed her. Before she could fathom that the event that occurred and understand what happened, he turned away. Biddy saw him vanish as though he were under an enchanting spell rising from the forbidden Dark Woods.

~

That night, Biddy could hardly sleep a wink. When she thought about the stranger in the next few days, her body would bubble in excitement and a smile crept onto her lips. Once her mother even noticed her smiling to herself and asked her why she was so happy, making Biddy's cheeks flush red. At night, she lay on her bed fidgeting, her body burning up with desire. She ached for his smile, to touch the ringlets of his hair, imagining what they might feel like. Her heart was pumping blood rapidly, and afraid her heart would scare off her body, she laid a hand on her torso. With a trembling palm she felt the throbbing reach her head and throb in her ears. Her stomach was in knots. She placed her pointer finger on her lip, remembering their kiss, and her excitement grew.

She was smiling from ear to ear, but then her face froze, as worry began to come over her. What if her mother or someone from the village discovered her folly? She would be forbidden from seeing him. Her mother would be hurt and be cross with her. The words of her grandmother echoed in the dark room. Villagers would frown at the little girl who, disobeyed their rules.

It was daylight and rays of sunshine bathed her bedroom, but Biddy felt a deep melancholy. She could not stomach any porridge, it hurt her to swallow. The promised hour arrived but her legs were weighed down like lead in her stockings. At the same time, her body felt light as air and her head was throbbing. As she drew closer to the place where she was to meet him, he was nowhere to be seen, and she began to worry. Would he not come as he'd promised? Biddy thought to herself. Had she come too early or late? Just then, he jumped out, frightening Biddy enough to make her trip and fall. He bent over laughing, holding his knees, and then reached out with his paw-like hand with the long sharp nails.

'Come on, pretty girl.' As she grew afraid, his face grew gentle 'Are you afraid of the woods?' he asked.

Biddy nodded timidly so he spoke very softly, 'Fear is of the unknown only until the unknown is known.' He smiled tilting his head down, and a ringlet of hair dangled near her face. He extended his large paw to her again, and held her small hand in his.

~

Afterwards, Biddy watched as he disappeared into the dark woods. She stood alone holding a rope of beautiful red and white flowers, just as he promised her they would find deep in the woods. It was a large field with patches of the sun's rays creeping through a thick canopy, where the flowers were white with splatters of red. She had gathered many, and as she started weaving them together, her fingers began to feel sticky with their viscous liquid.

Biddy now stood in the middle of the path, holding the rope of flowers in front of her. She then turned her head to the left where up ahead, beyond the cherry trees, lay her grandmother's cottage. She then turned to her right, where she could see her home, her village. As she stood there unmoving, flashes of blinking images went through her mind, which blended into a deep pain in her vulva. Scared, she started to run, pain shooting through her body, and sticky red liquid running down her legs.

~

Weeks had passed since her rendezvous with the big bad wolf. Biddy was curled up at the windowsill, gazing up at the pale sky. Her mother was mending her red hooded robe in her rocking chair. Her grandmother was no longer at the cottage at the edge of the wood. The day after her meeting with the wolf, the huntsman brought bad tidings to them: her grandmother's cottage had been ransacked. Only a bloody nightgown and cap had been found by the old lady's bedside. There were muddy paw prints everywhere.

And just that morning, a villager had brought more bad news. The huntsman had shot a grey wolf near their village, but on close inspection, he saw that the carcass was not a wolf, but an other animal—a human hybrid with pointy ears and yellow narrow eyes. Its irises were black as coal, it had two silver canine teeth, and pawed feet and hands. It was one of the wolf people, the youngest perhaps who had come down from the mountain. The villagers feared that if more came, the dark days would begin again.

A tear rolled down Biddy's cheek and she wondered if he'd come back for her that morning, or for something more sinister. A question with an answer she would never know. Dazed, she whispered a sad verse:

'*Come little children into the dark … Tra la la la la …*'

Biddy's mother's face froze, and her rocking halted. The song took her back to the dark red night of Biddy's birth. She closed her eyes and understood. She walked over to Biddy and put her arms around her daughter. She sighed gently, but her heart felt tight and uneasy, holding her child in a gentle embrace. She asked herself—would the never-ending story ever end? Biddy and her mother embraced each other, one protecting the other. They opened their eyes to a bright sunny day with mockingbirds chirping. Biddy's mother walked slowly back to her rocking chair and started to rock. Picking up the robe, she bent her head closer and continued stitching. The robe looked even brighter red, and the embroidered white calla lilies were tainted a deep crimson.

# The Witch

## *by Sharmila*

SINCE REACHING THE PALACE WITH JOSHAM THREE years ago, there had been nothing more shocking than his silence at today's dinner. True, he was disappointed after the cabinet meeting in the afternoon. But even after my repeated pleas, he didn't say anything. He did not even look at Sofia, our little butterfly.

Seeing her father returning from the meeting, his little butterfly walked towards him with joy, but Josham did not even notice her. He had never behaved like that before. He was reluctant to join the dinner, but he was not able to refuse when his mother herself came to call him. As expected, with a dry look and cold voice, she invited me too. Joining them for dinner has never been pleasant for me due to my fear of defying formal royal rules at the dining table. So, I have never been able to enjoy the delicacies.

Very rarely do I see all of them together. Every year, during the Sun Festival, all the family from different corners of the country

185

come to the palace to attend the cabinet meeting. My Josham is the second one among four children of the king and queen.

Princess Jovino, his elder sister, married a lord after the demise of his first wife. He had three children already, and she was not able to get pregnant with a man who was thirty years older than her. The lameness in the left leg was seen as a bad omen and the cause of infertility. Who knows who is sterile among them! Her husband is very egoistic and angry with everyone because he can't be the next king. Princess Jovino was discarded from the 'royal lineage' due to her disability, so her husband lost his chances of becoming king. Physical disability is a curse! Oh, what kind of people are here? But maybe that discrimination is what makes her so close to me. She alone creates a feeling of loving me from the bottom of her heart. But what makes her my favourite is her secret and the stealthy attempts to feed my Sofia from her dry breasts.

Josham has another sister and brother but they always keep their distance from me. Without realizing their deliberate attempts to avoid me in the earlier days, I tried to join them for a walk or a dance. It is horrible to even remember those moments now. Even when I became pregnant, neither of them took care of me. Jovino was there when I was giving birth to Sofia. Indeed, she was the one who took Sofia from my arms for the first time. Neither her grandma nor her other aunt ever came to my bedroom to see her. Even their maids were not supposed to talk to me.

Love and respect demand certain royal conditions in this palace. I do not fit those conditions and nor does Jovino. Jovino has become habituated to it now. She rarely speaks, and there is always a sadness visible in her eyes. But she has always stood with me. All the others were horrible—even the maids. Even though I was the wife of the future king, nobody treated me even as an ordinary human being. But most disgusting were their attempts to blame me for all the misfortunes of the country. They always made me feel like an outsider, but it is my love for my prince that gives me the strength to keep going.

~

Even though I had heard this 'witch Rapunzel' accusation before, what happened today at the dinner table was extreme. In front of the King and Queen, one of Josham's uncles referred to me as a witch. Nobody disagreed with him. Jovino tried to protest but she was silenced by the Queen. Guests can't be offended! How ridiculous! Guests can insult a family member, but nobody feels anything wrong has happened. And my husband … he was silent throughout. One by one, were all of them turning against me? Why do they believe I am a witch?

I left that gathering on the pretext of feeding Sofia. Our room is near the garden which borders the river Lima. Since more security was needed in the capital for the Sun Festival, all the soldiers had left the garden. It was so quiet in the room. Even the lamps seemed to give more shadows than light. I felt lonely. I really wished for Josham's presence. There is nothing more soothing than lying on his chest. But it was only after a long time that Josham came back to our room. Standing next to the cradle with teary eyes, I expected him to hold my hand and express support. But he did not even look at me. I wanted him to speak first; yet to overcome the awkward silence, I moved towards him and asked softly, 'My dear, where were you?'

He tried to avoid that question and moved towards the window. He looked at the mountaintops on the horizon. I went near him again. After all, he was my saviour, I couldn't leave him worried like this. I can't watch him worried, that too because of me. In those moments, if I had been a witch, I would have definitely saved him from this destiny with a magical spell. He was the soul of my happiness and my future as well. If I was becoming an issue for him,

I must address it. I hugged him from behind, held his hand with mine and said, 'My dear, I know you are worried, and I know the reasons too. But I am with you. Please talk to me. Let's discuss how we can solve this issue together.'

Looking into my eyes, finally, he uttered, 'It is complicated.'

I expected more from him, but he became silent again. 'Oh ... Is it about the witch in me? It is okay. That uncle has always rude to me.'

After a long silence, he spoke, 'To the contrary of what you understood, it is not about any witch in you. It is about power. The *throne*. You are a perfect excuse to keep me away from power.'

I responded in disbelief, 'The same reason for witch-hunting! How selfish are they? They all have power but still want the supreme power. They all want that throne.'

He again chose not to respond. He just kept looking away. I was becoming uncomfortable with his silence.

After a moment, taking his face between my hands, I spoke again, 'But my dear, you were already declared as the next King years before we met. Why is this unrest happening now?'

'They are going to revoke it.'

'REVOKE it? How can they? The promise taken at the altar of the Sun cannot be revoked!' I was finding it difficult to believe what I'd just heard him say.

'The King can. The king creates conventions to protect power. Or by offering seven goats to the Sun and bundles of gold to priests, anyone can revoke any promise here.' He thought for a while before he continued further.

'Here, the problem is not about any previous promise but about the present deliberations between those who are in power.' His tone, as well as his words, were becoming exceptionally clear, and he began to sound like a very elderly and experienced man.

'But for what? Because I am a witch or because I was from the forest or because I am without any palace or wealth to match your royal status?' I was becoming emotional. He was trying to become logical and less and less emotional. His concerns were evident; and on that scale, my daughter and I were weighing less.

'I am with you whatever happens and whoever is on the other side. And you were my king since you first appeared in front of me and I will be with you whatever you are.' Did he make a face at that? Let me be wrong.

'You are on my side … and what can that do? You just said that you have nothing. If you have nothing, what can you offer? How can you support or at least how can you defend me, Rapunzel?'

'What do I have other than you and your family? And I didn't cheat you by hiding anything. Or do you think so now?'

He didn't reply. He didn't even look at me. His eyes were elsewhere. His words, expressions, as well as his silence, were insulting.

Controlling my emotions, defying my self-esteem, I moved in front of him again. In a defensive tone, I said, 'Dear, I was in that forest before coming here as your wife. Even before that, I was in a tower when you saw me first. I was a prisoner when you proposed to me. I was left with no parents or ancestral property when you "decided" to kiss me.'

A sixth sense feeling of losing him started to grow inside me.

Moving towards Sofia's cradle, he became unexpectedly loud in his tone. 'Do you really think I believe all that you've told me about your past life? Do you think I am a fool who will believe that you survived there without any aid? That forest was full of wild creatures. And a tall tower without any door or stairs is ridiculous.'

I was shocked. Did he really say that? But why now? And how can he? There was a secret way to the tower, and he knew it well. And I was never alone in that forest. I had treated his wounds with the herbs and plants given to me by the forest-dwelling people. He knew that some of them visited me occasionally too.

'How cheap have you become, Josham? Is it after three years of living together you came to this realization? Now you are not only my husband but the father of our daughter too. Tell me straight. What do you want me to do?'

'Did I ask you to do anything? You need to do nothing. Stay away from me. Just leave me alone.'

'Leave you alone? Why? Because I am a witch? Or because your eligibility to become king is compromised due to me.' His looking away at this moment was the most disturbing.

Feeling suffocated due to his silence, I requested him, 'Josham, talk to me first. And ask the others to talk to me too. After all, I am the accused, not you. So how can they or you come to any judgment about me without even talking to me?'

'TALKING TO YOU! Women do not need to be consulted before making a judgment.' His reluctance to answer my questions was becoming evident.

'Then that is not judgment but bias. Hundreds of women were burnt in Europe for being witches and yet, not a single one of them was able to escape with their magical power. Witches without magic means they were not witches.' I was never so political in my statements, at least not in front of others.

'Then, what were they?'

'Josham, you know that they were not witches but ordinary women who protested against the abuse of lords and higher officials.' I suddenly wanted to say everything that I was unable to say for so long.

My words were making him angry. Yet, I continued speaking, 'To punish women, you invented this witchcraft. Do you know how many of these so-called witches were raped in your prisons?'

My fingers were targeting his face. I was becoming, without my knowledge, once again, the fighting forest girl.

'RAPUNZEL, shut up. They were witches. They had to be punished.' He fumbled while saying so.

He is losing the game. The truth will come out soon. Then I should decide whether to continue as an obedient wife or become a hanged witch or a fighting mother. I will not throw my Sofia to these power-mongering wolves. Sentence after sentence appeared in the slate of my mind.

In a more affirmative tone, I continued, 'By putting them in prison you all used them conveniently, then hanged to make them silent forever. And because they were not witches, they were not able to break those iron rods or turn you all into pigs.'

'Don't forget that these punishments were decided by the Queen, a mother of two daughters.' That was his last card.

I responded by saying, 'Power protects power, and once a woman becomes the queen, she too will speak the same language. She has to. That's why she became a queen.'

'Then, why are you different? You are powerful. You are the wife of the next king. Why did you become targeted and accused as a witch? The powerful are supposed to defend you, right?' I was laughing inside when he addressed me as the 'wife of the next king'.

I could see through his conspiracy. I was accused as a witch, and he was utilizing it for his own gain. Within hours I would be publicly denounced as a witch. And I was sure that Josham, my husband, who has not shown any sign of support so far, would not defend me.

'But I am not powerful. If you are not there to protect me, what power am I left with? Nobody will dare to touch a girl if Prince Josham is with her. Otherwise, I am only a witch-turned-woman, an unfortunate mother, brotherless, an orphan from the forest. I have nothing to offer. I am not among the powerful, Josham.' Even though my voice was quivering, I was fearless inside.

His expression was adamant. Why did my hero become so insulated to our love when his throne is taken away?

I was waiting for his response, but he moved to the wall and grabbed his sword. For a moment, I was scared. Why does he need a sword now?

I assured myself, 'He won't kill me.'

'Why do you need a sword right now?' I tried to be humble.

'Do I need to convince you, hmm?' He became louder.

I was not only afraid for my life, but worried for him as well.

To ease the tension, I tried my next and perhaps the last move. I held his arm, pushed the sword a little away and said in a mellow tone, 'No dear, not at all. But you didn't even look at our butterfly, Sofia. Can we sit together with her for some time?'

He looked at Sofia with a wooden face. That look was strong enough to make me realize that he was neither my hero nor my saviour anymore.

I looked at him for a moment and then shifted my gaze to Sofia, who was still sleeping unbothered by all the noise happening around her. I told myself, 'That is not her father. A father can't look at his daughter like that. I do not want such a father. I can raise her without the support of such a ruthless power-hungry man.'

Maybe he could sense what I was thinking, because his next words, 'I know how to love. I know how to show it. But don't come in between me and my goals.'

∽

I stood silent as Josham walked out of our room. With each of his receding footsteps, I told myself again and again, 'Josham has left my life.'

There are moments in life where you need to be loved and hugged, and those moments define your love. If he had walked away from that tower, like the many men who were afraid of my grandma, I wouldn't have gone searching for him in the forest later. Love needs expression.

I was feeling broken, but suddenly I realized that I only had a short time to escape.

I grabbed Sofia hurriedly. 'My daughter, we are leaving this palace.'

Suddenly awoken, she started crying. I kept talking even though I knew that my words might not make sense to her. 'Don't cry. You are not unlucky. A loving daughter is divine, but most people will go after cheaper things like a throne. Such people want fortified homes to guard themselves. You will live in the forest in the company of loving and caring people. I will take you there. Promise.' I went on speaking while covering her in the sheet she was sleeping on.

I rushed towards the door. But suddenly I moved backwards with the thought, 'But how to escape from this hell? Nobody is there to help me. There is no one here whom I can trust.'

I leaned on the wall feeling clueless about my next move.

I looked at Sofia. She was also watching the garden and the darkness outside. I took a deep breath and told myself silently, 'If none of it works out, I will jump into the river Lima, and she will take us to a safe shore.'

Before climbing out of the window, I looked back at my room again. For three years, I'd lived there with my Josham. Now it looked like a strange place.

∼

I was cautiously moving towards the garden when I heard a voice from the distant darkness of the passage, calling in a feeble tone, 'Rapunzel, wait …'

'Who is there?' I shivered in those cold winds.

'Jovino! What happened? Why are you gasping? Or are you shivering? Is there anybody after you?' I tried to be brave and normal seeing the face behind that unexpected voice.

She came nearer. She hugged me and kissed Sofia in a hurry and said, 'Where are you going now? It is not safe here. Come, we can go inside.'

I could sense that something was wrong. Or probably things had started to happen as expected. Otherwise, she would not have come here in the middle of the night. Even though I never saw her brave enough to make a bold move, this time, I felt something very different in her.

'Inside the palace, hmmm? Is it safer there?' I asked her while looking at her eyes and found her scared.

'I don't know where it is safe or whom to trust. But you are not safe.'

Something has definitely happened. Obviously, it was about me.

'Oh, come on, Jovino. What happened?' I asked her, but without waiting for her answer, I turned and moved towards the garden. I wanted to leave at the earliest.

She held my hand from behind and said in a heavy voice, 'No, no … don't go there. Please come to my room with me, please.'

She was pleading, and it meant a lot to me. I had a feeling that she could be trusted, but I preferred not to hurry to oblige. Instead, I decided to talk to her and understand her situation.

'Please don't worry about me. I am safe. You know that I am not an easy target. I am the wife of the future king.' I tried to pretend to relax despite knowing that I had to be quick.

I grabbed her hand and walked slowly to the other side of the garden.

To my surprise, guards were absent from the watchtowers. The torches too, were not lit, other than those by the riverside.

'We can't go to the garden. It is not safe there. Please come with me, we need to find Josham also. He isn't safe either.' Her voice was conveying her fear. She was scared like a rat in front of a snake.

I felt that it was the right time to ask her, 'Why are you scared? Why is Josham not safe?'

'I don't know what is happening. But my husband and his sons are planning to kill Josham. There are others with them too. And I heard them planning to blame it on you as witchcraft.' She was crying while she spoke.

Even though I expected to hear something like that, it was still a shock.

'Don't worry about Josham. He will defeat them in any fight. And about my witchcraft! Who will believe it?' I tried to feign ignorance about the events she'd mentioned.

'Everybody will believe it. Those who do not believe it will be next in line.' She sounded terrified and helpless but she carried on speaking, 'Rapunzel, it is not only a question about who will believe it but also about who will accuse you. You are unaware of the conspiracy going on in this royal family. Not only my husband and his children, but others too have decided similarly. That includes my parents.' She looked ashamed disclosing this reality.

'For years I have been a victim of their accusations. My lameness became the perfect reason for them to dump me. Even Josham did that to me.' She was relieving her pain by talking.

'Josham left you! Why? I heard priests wrote your destiny.'

'No priest would dare call the eldest daughter of the King a bad omen. I've had this lameness since birth but my family turned into a curse when I grew up.' Her tone was indicative of her hate towards them.

We both stood silent until I asked her, 'What do you want me to do? Why did you run to me?'

'I don't know how to say this. But ... give me Sofia. I will care for her as my own daughter. Please give her to me. Perhaps it is my selfishness talking, but there is nothing else I can do.' She tried to take Sofia from my arms while she spoke.

'And what about me?' I asked while looking straight into her eyes.'

'You? I don't know. Honestly, I am afraid for you. But soldiers will come after you soon'.

A clap of thunder exploded in the faraway skies. But I didn't hear it because of the loud voices inside me. All those quarrels and unnecessary accusations over all these years. I had never taken them seriously but I realized now that they were not innocent. I had never noticed Josham's ravenous hunger for the throne.

Jovino's touch brought me back to the present. She was waiting for my decision.

'Sister, I won't let others decide on my life.' I felt new courage in my words.

'Then what can you do? Who is with you? What will you do with Sofia tonight other than jumping into this water?'

I realized that this was the right moment to ask her to come with me. She would do that to be with Sofia.

'I am not going to jump into this water, and I am not going back to that cursed palace. I am Sofia's mother. I am going to ride over this river to give her a life. I am not going to die thanks to a cheating husband and his family of power-hungry criminals. I am going to live.'

In the most peaceful and courageous manner that I could muster, I held her close and asked, 'Do you want to come with me?'

She had not expected that, but she was also not going to refuse blindly.

'Jovino, what are you left with here? A loving husband or caring brothers or supporting parents?' I was firm in my tone.

She stood expressionless in front of me and kept looking at Sofia.

'What you had received in life so far was an insult and suffering. What else is awaiting you in that palace? Do you want to be a bad omen in everyone's eyes or a mother in Sofia's?'

Raindrops touched her pale face. Tears started to mix with the cold drops from the skies. She looked back at the palace. The silent and cold building didn't give her hope.

She looked back at Sofia. A brightness flashed through her face. Yes, it was the right moment to act. I gave her my child, and she hugged Sofia to her chest.

'Get into a raft.' I said as I went to each torch around the river to kill its light. It was tiring, but now there was perfect darkness. Nobody from the palace could trace any movement there. Then, I started to untie all the other rafts. All of them left the shore and disappeared into the river.

Jovino was shivering, but she kept Sofia wrapped inside her blouse. I put the blanket around her and took the paddle in my hand. With all my effort, I began rowing through the deep water. After a long silence, Jovino spoke. Holding Sofia tightly, she said, 'The cold is rising. And seeing this water, I feel scared for her.'

'There is nothing warmer than a mother's love. She will be safe with you.' I smiled and urged the raft forward with more passion and determination. Even the tides seemed to support us.

# About the Anthology Process

THE PROCESS OF COLLECTING THESE STORIES BEGAN in 2020, during the first wave of the COVID-19 pandemic, when Rising Flame invited applications for an online writing workshop for women with disabilities. Eighteen finalists participated in a five-month fiction writing workshop and feedback process with author and poet Aditi Rao. The spaces created virtually for this workshop were fully accessible and inclusive, with sign language interpreters and live captioners and a respectful, accepting environment where screen time offs and quiet times were accepted and worked with. The workshop intended to impart the craft and skill of writing but also lead the process of self-reflection, voicing, and healing, all important steps to empowerment.

The thirteen completed stories that came out of this process are written by authors from India and Sri Lanka, representing a range of regional contexts and disabilities, including visual, hearing and locomotor disabilities, as well as autism, psychosocial disabilities and attention-deficit hyperactivity disorder. The completed drafts of the stories they wrote then were edited by writer and editor Richa Kaul Padte over twelve months.

# About the Organization

RISING FLAME IS A NATIONAL AWARD-WINNING NON-profit organization based in India, working for recognition, protection and promotion of human rights of people with disabilities, particularly women and youth with disabilities. Rising Flame's vision is to build an inclusive world in which diverse bodies, minds and voices thrive with dignity; live free of discrimination, abuse and violence; and enjoy equal opportunities and access. Since its establishment in 2017 as an organization led by women and persons with disabilities, it aims to enable persons with disabilities standing at multiple intersections to have a voice, have a space, be heard and lead from the front. The organization has a two-fold strategy—to build capacities of persons with disabilities and to influence the ecosystem. It's major programmes are on leadership, mental health, sexual and reproductive health, gender based violence, research and policy influence. Rising Flame is known for its groundbreaking research Neglected and Forgotten—the first report across the world capturing the impact of the COVID-19 crisis on lives of women with disabilities. In 2023, Rising Flame also led the work in over twenty countries on disability, equity, justice in India's G20 presidency. Rising Flame is committed to advancing rights while upholding disability justice and feminist principles. Website: www.risingflame.org. Socials: @risingflamenow

# Acknowledgements

T HE PROJECT 'MY TALE TOO' LAUNCHED BY RISING
Flame translated into this heart-warming anthology and
was launched to mainstream disabled realities through
popular tales. The project was envisioned and conceptualized by
Nidhi Ashok Goyal, Founder and Executive Director of Rising
Flame. The seeds of this were planted and nurtured by Nidhi's own
experiences as a woman with a disability and her deep work with
persons with disabilities over the years.

The foundations of this book were laid in the 'My Tale Too'
writing workshop hosted by Rising Flame in 2020. It was created as
a response to the lack of representation of women with disabilities
in fairy tales. Aditi Rao, poet and writer, played the instrumental
role of designing and facilitating the workshop and provided writers
with the skills and structure for narrating their stories. Over a period
of twelve months, Richa Kaul Padte, writer and editor, provided
in-depth editorial feedback to strengthen each of these stories. The
entire process from applications to publishing was driven by Rising
Flame's Co-Lead, Programmes, Srinidhi Raghavan.

The workshops were executed with the support of Rising Flame staff Arjita Mital and Chayanika Iyer and made accessible with the support of live transcriptionists: Teesta, Fizza, Kunjika and Roshni and the Indian Sign Language interpretation team at ISLIA. Without their work, the workshops and the process of editing and feedback would not have been fully accessible and inclusive.

We are grateful to Sohini Basak, former commissioning editor at HarperCollins Publishers for seeing its need and potential and commissioning it.

The book was possible only because of the dedication, commitment and voices of all the women with disabilities who participated in the workshop, who spent months working on their stories and stayed with us from inception to publication. We admire them for their courage in bringing vulnerability and joy in their writings, and for nudging the world to think of alternate realities. We are forever grateful to them for their tenacity and willingness to embark on this journey with us.

# About the Authors

**Kanika Agarwal**

Kanika lost her hearing at the age of ten and grew up surrounded by hearing people. Her first encounter with the deaf community happened in her early teens. She was bewildered by this new world and happy to be a part of it. Education has always been her passion, and entry into the deaf world helped her develop a penchant for deaf education. Today, she is a known face throughout India in the field of deaf education and her students love her for her student-centric ways of teaching. She is also the first deaf TEDx speaker in India, who gave her talk in Indian sign language. Kanika hopes to use her skills for the betterment of deaf education in India and to see deaf children on a par with other children from all walks of life.

**Nidhi Ashok Goyal** is the Founder and Executive Director of the leading National Award-winning non-profit organization Rising Flame, pioneering work on leadership and rights of women and persons with disabilities in India. She has been working on disability rights and gender justice for the past thirteen years at the global, national and grassroots levels through research, writing, training, policy influence and art. Her work has created impact in five continents and in over thirty countries.

A disability, diversity and inclusion specialist, she has advised, led and steered numerous global and national organizations and initiatives. Recently, she led disability inclusion as steering committee member and working group lead in more than twenty countries in Civil 20, during India's G20 presidency. She has been appointed to the core group of Persons with Disabilities by the National Human Rights Commission India, is on the Diversity and Inclusion Task Force of the Federation of Indian Chambers of Commerce and Industry, is the governing body member of ADD India, and sits on the advisory board of Voice—a grant-making project by the Dutch ministry. She has led multistakeholder and cross-movement work, influenced policies and systems, and authored groundbreaking research, all with a vision to foster inclusion of women and youth with disabilities within India and globally. She has steered a leading global women's rights organization—AWID—as the youngest and first-ever disabled president, and made huge strides in inclusion as the former global advisor to the UN Women's Executive Director. From local to global, she is an influential public voice and has spoken at many political and prestigious spaces like European Development Days, United Nations Conference of the States Parties, Commission for Status of women, Dutch Ministry linking and learning events, UNFPA regional leadership  meet, US consulate, Ford Foundation, and other governmental and corporate spaces. She is also India's first female disabled comedian and uses humour to challenge stereotypes around disability gender and sexuality. Her leadership and work have been appreciated and awarded by the Government of India, FICCI YFlo, Indira University, National

Association for the Blind, ABP News and Sur Optimist Mumbai, amongst others. You can follow her work @saysnidhigoyal

**Niluka Gunawardena** is an educator, researcher and activist based in Colombo, Sri Lanka. Her understanding of disability is informed by her experience of multiple disabilities and intersectionality.

Niluka earned a Master of Arts degree in Disability and Gender (with Distinction) from the University of Leeds, UK. She is a visiting lecturer in Disability Studies at the University of Kelaniya and the University of Colombo. She is a consultant to the AHEAD project conducted by the Centre for Disability Education, Research and Practice to create an accessible and inclusive learning environment for all students at the University of Colombo. She is on the teaching team of CREA's Disability, Sexuality and Rights Online Institute and SGRI. She has taught geography and earth science to secondary school students for several years and is currently working on introducing mindfulness to schools in association with Mindful Educators.

Niluka regularly conducts community and corporate training workshops on disability awareness and rights. She is a researcher who has worked on evidence-based policy for organizations like the Human Environment Research Observatory, Equal Ground and BBC. She serves on the advisory committees of Arrow, HYPE Sri Lanka and LIRNEasia among others.

**O Aishwarya** has a Master's degree in Development from Azim Premji University and is currently pursuing Doctoral studies at IIT Bangalore in the area of IT and Society. She has worked for a year at Vision Empower, a non-profit organization that aims to make science, technology, engineering and mathematics (STEM) subjects accessible to blind and visually impaired children studying in special schools in Karnataka. She is an avid reader, and an occasional novice writer. Having recently discovered ways of producing visual art as a blind person, she is now exploring the use of art as a medium for breaking stereotypes and confronting ableism. Researching, and creating more knowledge on disability studies and accessibility, is her passion as well as profession.

**Dr P. Karkuzhali** is Assistant Professor, Department of English, Chellammal Women's College of the Pachaiyappa's Trust, University of Madras, Chennai. She is the co-editor of *Unearthing the Unexplored: A Critical Companion to Fourth World Literature* (2016) and *Subalternity and Literature* (2017). She is the editor-in-chief of *The Text* (ISSN: 2581-9526), an international peer-reviewed online journal of language, literature and critical theory.

One of her research articles titled 'Tamil Folk Music: Rewriting Dalit Identity in K.A. Gunasekaran's *The Scar*' has been published in *Indian Literature*, Sahitya Akademi's bi-monthly journal (Sept/Aug 2019). Her research interests include postcolonial/indigenous literature and subaltern/disability studies. She writes poetry in Tamil. She is the author of *Enna Saaral* (2019). She is the recipient of the Kasthuri Ramnath State Award, the Hellen Keller State Award, the Wisdom Award, and the Rev. Fr. Lawrence Sundaram Gold Medal for outstanding performance in the Doctor of Philosophy in English.

**Parita Dholakia** is a Mumbai-based late-deafened adult. She is a health communicator by profession, an A11y Tech Crusader by passion, and a Rare Disease Sufferer by genetics. Born as a blue baby, and later diagnosed with osteogenesis imperfecta, her teenage years were a blur between fractures and hospitals. Later, she saw the greener grass of the developed lands and finished her education, but while still trying for a podium finish in life, she got hit by a progressive hearing loss. By utilizing her triad perspectives of having had normal hearing, being hard of hearing, and now deaf, she aspires to continue raising awareness about late-developed and invisible disabilities. She is currently working in a pharma company in Mumbai.

**Priyangee Guha** is a lawyer, researcher, policy analyst, trainer and human rights activist. In the decade of her legal career, she has developed an interest in reformative justice, healing and creating better legal and social response systems to violence in our society. She works with victims of violence in India. Throughout her career, she has responded to over 500 victim–survivors of violence and provided social, legal and emotional support. As part of the Counsel to Secure Justice, she has represented victim–survivors of sexual abuse for three years in court. As an independent consultant, she has also created easy-to-read leaflets on child rights for the National Commission for Protection of Child Rights (NCPCR). As a part of the Centre for Equity Studies, she has designed modules which are widely used to make law accessible to children, adults and those disenfranchised by the law. She has conducted hundreds of training programmes for lawyers, social workers, police officers, school principals and teachers on the essential tenets of the Juvenile Justice Act in India, laws related to sexual abuse of children, human trafficking, right to education, and prevention of sexual harassment in the workplace. She has written for publications including *The Indian Express*, *The News Minute*, Wikimedia, *Point of View*, *DailyO*, *Restorative Justice: Strategies for Change Ireland*, Broadsheet.ie, Rising Flame, *Funny Women*, Population First and more. Her writing spans the criminal justice system, the impact of working with victims of violence, and the rights of persons with disabilities. She participates in panels, webinars and conferences where she talks about the justice system where the response is centred on healing and not vengeance.

She has been actively undertaking research on protecting children from violence and understanding the impact of COVID-19 on disabled women. In addition, she is a registered solemnizer with the Department of Social Protection, Ireland. She moonlights as a comedian and performs live in comedy clubs in Ireland.

**Rakshita** is an educator and consultant for disability rights organizations and schools. She has a master's in intellectual and developmental disabilities from the University of Kent, UK. She has extensive experience as a teacher in both general education and special education. She is a member of two international advocacy organizations: NeuroClastic, Inc. and Universal Design for Learning: Special Interest Group. She has also presented at multiple national and international conferences. She is passionate about pedagogy, autism and inclusion. Her approach is centred on developing good mental health in disabled children. Being autistic, she ardently advocates for autistic children and adults through her poetry, essays, talks and training programmes. She hopes to teach the society that they can and must rely on disabled people to solve the world's biggest problems. She dreams of a world where all live and let live.

**Sanchita Ain** is an Advocate-on-Record in the Supreme Court of India. With experience of almost a decade in the field of law, she has handled complex matters before the Supreme Court, High Courts, and other forums in the country. These include landmark constitutional law cases like linking of PAN with Aadhaar, triple talaq, affirmative action, rights of minority institutions, land acquisition cases, the 2G spectrum case, and matters relating to civil, corporate, competition, service and family laws. Being recognized as a disability rights expert by the legal fraternity, she has appeared as an amicus in a landmark case on the right to reasonable accommodation. Her recent endeavour includes successfully arguing the issue of accessibility of digital education for students with disabilities, leading to the formation of inter-ministerial committees and several sub-committees being constituted under the directions of the Hon'ble Supreme Court to look into the issue. Sanchita Ain holds the prestigious LLM degree in International Human Rights Law with distinction from the University of Essex. She works extensively in the area of gender and disability issues and has delivered lectures and participated in several gender- and disability-related sensitization drives across the country.

**Sarani** was raised in the island paradise of Sri Lanka, and for the past three years she has been in the United Kingdom by herself. With multiple learning disabilities, moving to a new country was challenging and overwhelming. All of this has been a huge learning for her as she can now say that she is beginning to understand the gifts of her multiple learning difficulties. Earlier she felt ashamed and had many regrets because of all the years she spent being angry at being born like this. But along this long difficult road, at one point, she was left homeless, during the early days of the pandemic and it changed her. It could be because of her ADHD, but she believes that 'it ain't over till the fat lady sings'. She adds to this: even after the fat lady sings and falls over and dies, don't throw the towel in, for any one with a disability, physical or learning, life is that much harder to push through and many times one feels too overwhelmed to move forward. At forty, she feels she is truly starting to know who she is. But the rose that blooms late is more newsworthy than the one among the 100,000 roses that bloom in springtime.

**Sharmila Rathee** is a teacher educator at the University of Delhi. Born with a congenital disability in her right hand, her interest lies in the field of inclusive education and disability studies. She loves to drive, travel, write children's books and spend time in the lap of nature.

**Somrita Urni Ganguly** is a professor, poet and literary translator. She was a Fulbright Doctoral Research Fellow at Brown University, and is an alumna of the University of East Anglia's International Literary Translation and Creative Writing Summer School. She served as a judge for the PEN America Translation Prize, and an Expert Reader for the English PEN Translation Grant, the National Translation Award (USA), and the National Endowment for the Arts Translation Grant offered by the US federal government. Somrita is currently Head of the Department of English, Maharaja Manindra Chandra College, University of Calcutta, and has co-founded The Writing Programme in India. Her work has been showcased at the London Book Fair, and she has read in cities like Bloomington, Mumbai, Boston, Kolkata, Cove, Delhi, Hyderabad, London, Miami, Providence and Singapore. She has delivered lectures and presented her work at several institutes around the world including the University of Pennsylvania, Princeton University, the National University of Singapore, Bath Spa University, the Emily Dickinson Museum, the American Literary Translators Association, the Oregon Society of Translators and Interpreters and the University of Nottingham. Somrita edited an anthology of food poems, *Quesadilla and Other Adventures* (2019), and translated *3 Stories: Sarat Chandra Chattopadhyay* (2021), *Firesongs* (2019), *Shakuni* (2019), and *The Midnight Sun: Love Lyrics and Farewell Songs* (2018), among other works.

**Soumita** is a solution finder. That's what took her on the path of social entrepreneurship. She is a pioneer in the field of inclusive fashion and runs her own line of inclusive clothing, Zyenika Inclusive Fashion, where the designs are adapted to people's body types, physical requirements and challenges. She was motivated to do this from her lived experience after losing mobility at thirty-one due to an autoimmune disorder. At one point she was completely bedridden. Now, she operates with 20 per cent mobility. For nearly two decades, she has worked on various development issues—with a particular focus on health, livelihoods and governance. Her work has taken her to villages and cities across India, where she learnt more about indigenous innovations. She has been awarded the UNDP-supported Global HoneyBee Creative and Inclusive Innovations Award, 2020 and Best Business Idea Award at Breaking the Glass Ceiling, 2021, US Consulate, Kolkata. Soumita started her career as a freelance journalist during her collegiate days as a sociology undergrad at the University of Calcutta. Later she worked as a broadcast journalist before turning to a career in action research informing innovations and policies for social development. She holds a Master's in Development Studies from the International Institute of Social Sciences, The Hague, and a Postgraduate Diploma in Journalism from the Asian College of Journalism.

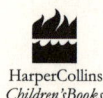

![HarperCollins logo] **HarperCollins** *Publishers* India

At HarperCollins India, we believe in telling the best stories and finding the widest readership for our books in every format possible. We started publishing in 1992; a great deal has changed since then, but what has remained constant is the passion with which our authors write their books, the love with which readers receive them, and the sheer joy and excitement that we as publishers feel in being a part of the publishing process.

Over the years, we've had the pleasure of publishing some of the finest writing from the subcontinent and around the world, including several award-winning titles and some of the biggest bestsellers in India's publishing history. But nothing has meant more to us than the fact that millions of people have read the books we published, and that somewhere, a book of ours might have made a difference.

As we look to the future, we go back to that one word— a word which has been a driving force for us all these years.

Read.

Harper Collins    4th    HARPER PERENNIAL    HARPER BUSINESS    HARPER BLACK    हार्पर हिन्दी

HarperCollins *Children'sBooks*    HARPER DESIGN    HARPER VANTAGE    Harper Sport